She ignored the sen... to think about and ... the tiny newborn. T...

She allowed the relief of Simon's skills to flow over her. And the tension in her shoulders and neck released even more. The responsibility shifted to the man beside her. Simon Purdy had this all under control. She could relax.

He was here and, surprise, surprise, finally treating her the same as he treated the other staff.

She thought about that. No. No. Actually, he was treating her like she was the relative of one of the patients. With reassurance and an unspoken promise to do his best. And yet there was professional appreciation for her, there as well. She'd seen a shimmer of it before when they were working together, but it was a little hard to feel greatly appreciated if the person you worked with didn't speak to you.

If her niece wasn't so fragile, she'd be thinking all her Christmases had come at once.

Dear Reader,

I loved the chance to spend a little more time with Malachi and Lisandra and the twins from the last book, *Father for the Midwife's Twins*, as in this story, they help their friends find love.

In some ways, this is an enemies-to-lovers story! Simon and Isabella do not get off on the right foot because they're both afraid to trust.

I loved Isabella. She's a wonderful character—strong, intelligent and caring despite some difficult relationships with men, including her workaholic father. But what she really needs, however, is a loving partner—though she doesn't know this yet.

It's no surprise that Simon finds her irresistible. Simon is such a heartthrob and impossible not to love! His path to love is not easy because since the death of his mother and his wife and child, he doesn't believe he has the power to protect the women around him. Instead, he finds his power and self-esteem from protecting his patients, which makes him incredibly committed to his job—a double-edged sword for Isabella!

I hope you love Simon and Isabella's story as much as I do. Wishing you a big happy smile at the end.

Love,

Fi xx

If you purchased this book without a cover you should be aware that this book is stolen property. It was reported as "unsold and destroyed" to the publisher, and neither the author nor the publisher has received any payment for this "stripped book."

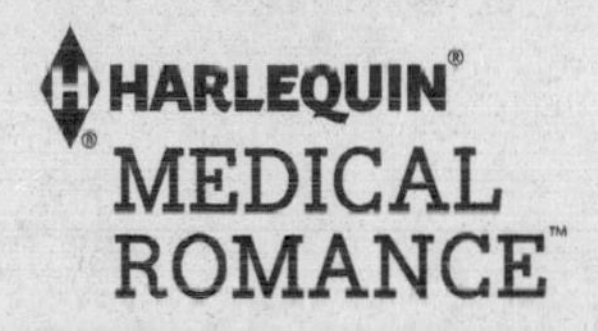

Recycling programs for this product may not exist in your area.

ISBN-13: 978-1-335-59529-4

Healing the Baby Doc's Heart

Copyright © 2024 by Fiona McArthur

All rights reserved. No part of this book may be used or reproduced in any manner whatsoever without written permission except in the case of brief quotations embodied in critical articles and reviews.

This is a work of fiction. Names, characters, places and incidents are either the product of the author's imagination or are used fictitiously. Any resemblance to actual persons, living or dead, businesses, companies, events or locales is entirely coincidental.

For questions and comments about the quality of this book, please contact us at CustomerService@Harlequin.com.

Harlequin Enterprises ULC
22 Adelaide St. West, 41st Floor
Toronto, Ontario M5H 4E3, Canada
www.Harlequin.com

Printed in U.S.A.

HEALING THE BABY DOC'S HEART

FIONA MCARTHUR

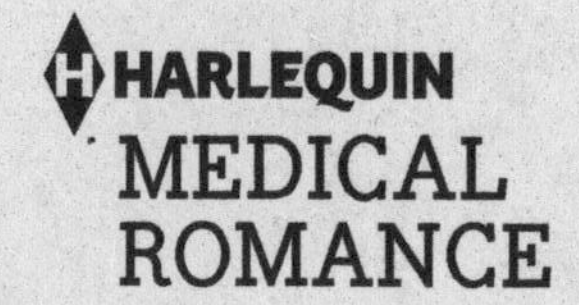

Fiona McArthur is an Australian midwife who lives in the country and loves to dream. Writing medical romance gives Fiona the chance to write about all the wonderful aspects of romance, adventure, medicine and the midwifery she feels so passionate about. When she's not catching babies, Fiona and her husband, Ian, are off to meet new people, see new places and have wonderful adventures. Drop in and say hi at Fiona's website, fionamcarthurauthor.com.

Books by Fiona McArthur

Harlequin Medical Romance

The Midwives of Lighthouse Bay

A Month to Marry the Midwife
Healed by the Midwife's Kiss
The Midwife's Secret Child

Christmas in Lyrebird Lake

Midwife's Christmas Proposal
Midwife's Mistletoe Baby

Christmas with Her Ex
Second Chance in Barcelona
Taking a Chance on the Best Man
Father for the Midwife's Twins

Visit the Author Profile page at Harlequin.com for more titles.

Dedicated to Jodie and her babies.

Praise for
Fiona McArthur

"I absolutely adored the story…. Highly recommended for fans of contemporary romance. I look forward to reading more of Fiona McArthur's work."

—*Goodreads* on *Healed by the Midwife's Kiss*

PROLOGUE

Vietnam, the first of May

ISABELLA HARGRAVES PULLED aside the curtains and looked down to the waking Hanoi street, seven floors below.

Warm air swirled around her fingers as she cracked open the window, yet the sky still radiated a pink glow from dawn. Her favourite time. Another hot day was coming.

An elderly vendor peddled below on a push-bike laden with multi-sized straw hats. These conical woven workers' hats could be seen in fields, sampans, on cyclists, and on the heads of tourists. On this pushbike, the towers of plaited straw rose behind the rider and out sideways, so he was encased in a cage of hats. He'd be on his way to sell them in the old quarter of the city.

One of Isabella's highlights for people-watching in Vietnam was noting the piles of drums, ladders, picture frames—in fact anything—on the back and front of push-bikes. Once she'd even seen a cow on a trailer pulled along by a motorcycle.

Nine million people and three million motorcycles. Such a crazy, wonderful place to live and work.

Of course, if you wanted to cross the road only a percentage of traffic would stop, and you needed to take your life in your hands. The trick, she'd found, was to walk slowly—no dashing—hand out, eyes open, and *voila*, the traffic avoided you. That was the local theory, anyway, and when she followed that it seemed to work.

From her window she could just see the pink sky lighting Hoen Kiem, the Lake of the Returned Sword, where an emperor had been said to use a magical sword to defeat the Ming Dynasty from China. The legends here fascinated her.

In this story, after victory, the Golden Turtle god had returned the sword to the bottom of the lake, and today the Turtle Tower stood on its own tiny island, on guard, as if to keep an eye out for the endangered turtles that were swimming in the lake.

Isabella pulled on her runners so she could circle the expanse of still water in the early morning before she went to the maternity wing of the Old City Hospital.

Circumnavigating the lake on the winding paths at daybreak had become Isabella's favourite start to the day. The streets were quiet, and the pleasure of watching groups of women on the grassed foreshore, line-dancing to boom boxes, bickering over which song to play and the exuberance once decided, seemed to bring some of their infectious joy her way.

She and her partner Conlon had another month of secondment here. She'd loved every second so far. Loved sharing it with Conlon. She'd even begun to hope she'd found a partner in life after she'd been alone for so long. Conlon had suggested she should become a full-time academic instead of fitting her research in blocks between her nursing work as an intensivist.

Her mood dipped. Yesterday's emergency in the neonatal intensive care unit—or NICU—had required all her skills to assist in saving the first-born son of a woman she'd befriended, and though she'd been present in the unit only for research, it had been her skills from the other part of her life that had helped to save the baby.

Isabella, an expert in the field, had been invited to participate in a study of neonatal outcomes for premature babies. Conlon, an ambitious lecturer at Sydney University, had been so eager to co-author the paper she was writing that he'd asked to join her. Their relationship had become more than collegial, and he now shared the flat she'd rented.

She was still getting used to the fact that Conlon had said he was there for her. It seemed hard to believe when she'd been let down so often by her father's work priorities while she was growing up. It had felt as if every single time she'd needed him that her father had been elsewhere, working.

Her phone rang and she glanced down to see the caller ID. Speak of the devil. Her brows furrowed. Dad? Six a.m. here… It would be nine in the morning in Australia.

Suddenly she felt as if she were a motherless seven-year-old seeking an elusive hug, not a woman of twenty-seven.

She could count on the fingers of one hand how many times her father had rung her in the last year. Messages were usually sent via his very busy secretary at the Sydney Central Neurology Department.

A feeling of foreboding crept up her neck and circled her throat—because the last time he'd phoned had been to tell her about her brother-in-law's car accident, six months ago.

'Dad?'

'Isabella. I have bad news.'

No sugar coating. No, *How are you*? No, *I'm sorry to say this.* Not from Dad.

She felt her stomach roil with sick fear.

Was her widowed sister sick? Was it Nadia's pregnancy? The baby?

'It's your grandmother.'

Gran! The woman who had made up for the loss of her mother so long ago. The loss of her father, too, really. Because he'd morphed into a machine after Mum had died, and had only become more mechanical in his affections.

No. It couldn't be. Not Gran.

'An accident. Hit and run in Coolangatta. She's unconscious,' he went on. 'I don't believe she'll wake.'

Isabella closed her eyes as horror and the wash

of devastation began to saturate her insides along with cold fear.

'Isabella? Hello? Are you there?'

She jumped at the tone in her father's voice. 'Yes, sorry. I'm just trying to take it in. I'll come home, of course.'

'What?' she heard him snap. 'Why? There's nothing you can do.' His tone disbelieving. Sharp. Emphatic. 'No need. No. You must finish your work.' She heard the cold and clinical man for whom the god Work meant everything.

Her grandmother lay dying. Unconscious in hospital. Isabella wasn't leaving her alone.

'Of course there's something I can do. I can be with her. And with Nadia.'

Her father hmphed with exasperation. 'Your grandmother's not going to know you're with her.'

There it was. The impatience she'd grown up with. The inhuman being who was her father. He was probably already thinking about his next task.

'She's comatose. It's very sad. However, as I've said, it's unlikely she's going to regain consciousness.'

'I'm coming home.'

Or at least not home. Not to the cold, empty mausoleum her father lived in.

'I'll go to the Gold Coast. Be with Nadia. Stay at Gran's flat.'

I will talk to my grandmother even if she's unconscious.

It might help. Her grandmother might hear her at any point. Isabella would be there when she woke up.

Oh, Gran.

He huffed. 'You do what you need to do—though I can't imagine Conlon will be happy if you leave.'

She tilted her head at that. 'Conlon will come with me. Be with me. He'll support me.'

'Really? You both went there to do a job. Conlon knows your work is important and it's not finished. You should both stay.'

'We'll go back to Australia early. Come back to Vietnam later.'

Of course he'll come with me...support me.

God, she wanted him now, his arms around her, but he was already out jogging around the lake.

'I don't think you should. Nadia's there. She'll keep you up to date.'

She could almost imagine her father looking at his watch. Thinking he'd wasted enough time on this call.

'Thank you for ringing.'

And not getting your secretary to do it.

Isabella's fingers felt numb. Her lips clumsy as she said goodbye.

Gran...

A flash of sympathy for her father pierced her before he could hang up. 'Dad. Are you okay? Gran's your mother...'

'I'm sorry it's happened, of course.' He was silent for a moment. As if he was actually going to say he was upset. But no. 'There's nothing we can do. Your grandmother is eighty. She's had a good life.'

And then he was gone.

At first Isabella walked around the room in circles, picking things up and putting them down, trying to work out what to do. Trying to grasp the enormity of Gran lying in a hospital thousands of miles away. Alone. Possibly dying.

She thought about how much life, and love and laughter her grandmother had left inside her. Gran *had* to wake up. She couldn't bear the thought that her grandmother wouldn't be there. Wouldn't see Nadia's baby born.

The Sydney flights didn't leave until six p.m. from Hanoi to Singapore. And then a few hours later from Singapore to Sydney. They'd have to catch a domestic flight from Sydney to Brisbane and hire a car to drive to the Gold Coast. She'd arrange for her own car to be shipped up.

She thought of her sister. Alone in this. Poor Nadia… Six months pregnant and now she'd be losing two people she loved. Nadia needed her, too. No. Gran wouldn't die. She'd phone her as soon as she spoke to Conlon.

The door opened and Conlon breezed in from his run, bringing the heat from the pavements outside. His jet-black hair lay plastered to the sweat across his brows, which creased when he saw her face.

His long legs crossed the room to her quickly. 'What's wrong?'

She wasn't alone. Too many times in her childhood she and her sister had been alone…until Gran had stepped in. Thank goodness Conlon was here.

'My grandmother. She's in a coma. Hit and run in Coolangatta. We'll have to go back to Australia.' She reached forward and took his hand. 'We have to go home.'

He stared. 'I'm sorry… Run that by me again?'

How could he not have understood her?

She tamped down her impatience. 'My grandmother has been involved in an accident. I have to go home. I'll tell them we have to postpone our study. Put a hold on the paper.'

'Of course you have to go. But what do you mean, we have to postpone? We need to finish the project.'

He shook his head.

'I'm going home.'

'I know. I heard that. Your grandmother. You're fond of her.'

Fond? The word sat oddly.

'I'm terrified my grandmother is going to die,' she said slowly. Familiar dread was coiling inside her chest. 'I need you right now. You'll support me…?'

She hadn't meant to make it a question but it was too late now. She trailed off, looked at his face. Saw the truth. The distance that had grown between them in just minutes. That's all it took. Saw the selfishness she'd tried to ignore in all those little daily moments. Saw her father.

Conlon was looking past her, his gaze shifting away. He gave a more emphatic shake of his head this time.

'I'm not going to be any help. I'll stay and finish the project.'

This wasn't happening.

'They'll understand…we can come back. You don't need—'

He cut her off. 'No, it will only take a month for me to finish it. You go. Do what you have to do. Then come back if you can make it in time. If you can't, I'll tie it all up.' His chin went up. 'I'll still add your name on the paper.'

She shifted again at that. It had been her paper and she'd invited him to join her. He'd asked her to let him join. Now he was going to 'add her name' on it when she'd done eighty percent of the work?

She shook her head. Stung. Disgusted, actually. She narrowed her eyes as he avoided hers. But that was just work. Stuff to think on later. Later—when Gran was well. This was not important now.

Isabella shook her head. 'You're not listening to me. I want you to come and be with me. Support me. What if she dies?'

She knew she sounded forlorn and lost, and she hated it.

His face was screwed up, incredulous. 'You've flown alone more than I have. You'll be fine.' He waved a hand and glanced at his watch as it moved past his face. 'I'd better get moving.'

Isabella felt sick. And stupid. 'I don't want protection. I want support. There's a difference.'

'I would. If this was finished. But this work is too important, Isabella.'

She winced. Hurt. 'And I'm not?'

He'd already turned towards the bedroom. 'Don't be petty. Of course you're important. But I think you're not thinking right. Not thinking of our work. You're prioritising all wrong.'

Had he really just said that? Red-hot anger flooded through her. She could almost imagine her blood boiling like lava. Her father's favourite word all through her childhood. At school events and award nights. He was unable to come because he was 'prioritising'.

Conlon turned back briefly, oblivious to the fact that he wasn't in the right. 'Ridiculous for me to come with you. We're so close to finishing. This will be a breakthrough paper. Give us excellent credibility behind us.'

Through gritted teeth she whispered, 'My grandmother is dying.'

Oh, God. She saw it then. Why? Why was she attracted to these men who put work in front of everything? Like her father. She'd thought Conlon was safe. He was an academic, so at least he had no urgent calls taking him back to the hospital night after night. She'd thought—foolish her—that during every event or crisis, he would be there. For her. Would want to be.

If it hadn't been for Gran, she and Nadia wouldn't even have had a childhood. They would have spent their holidays locked in the house with part-time servants instead of going to visit Gran and flying up to her at the weekends when they were older.

And she'd thought she could make a life with Conlon. Thought they wanted the same things. Thought they'd be a caring family.

Idiot.

She'd have spent her life waiting for scraps of attention that didn't involve work. Just like in her childhood.

But she couldn't think about that now.

She said dully, 'You go and shower. When you come home I'll be gone.'

'Of course. That's fine. I'll give you a ring.'

Wow. So generous. Thoughtful.

Very quietly and clearly she said, 'No, don't bother.'

Conlon's dark brows drew together. He was irritated. His turn to be impatient. 'You're being foolish. We're good together. Our work is amazing.'

'*My* work is amazing.'

Because she was the one who found it easy. Made the connections and garnered the interviews that clarified the answers. She had a way with equations, and probabilities, always finding the right questions and writing everything down in the right words.

Conlon had let her down.

Hell, he couldn't even take the time to give her a hug of sympathy. What had she been thinking to attach herself to a man who was so like her father she'd have been starved for affection for the rest of her life?

Her heart wasn't broken—bruised, maybe—but her pride had taken a blow that had left her reeling.

She'd loved her time in Vietnam, had been honoured by the openness of the midwives and neonatal nurses she'd interviewed for her thesis. She'd ached over their stories, and enjoyed learning about a culture that was so different from her own. But she'd been here with Conlon and had thought something had been growing between them.

He'd been so enthusiastic about her scientific paper, and his handsome face had promised her a wonderful future at home and at work. She'd not seen what was now so obvious—that the man was selfish and egotistical.

Wow. Remembered his comment about the

paper. Seemed he thought it was generous that he'd let her share credit for her own thesis.

She'd almost loved him—or the man she'd thought he was—but now, as he turned to shower and change for the hospital, she felt as hollow and cast off as she'd felt as a child, when her father had immersed himself in his high-powered job.

She'd thought she'd got over that. Her gran would have scolded her for being dramatic. Would've said Conlon had done her a favour, exposing his shortfalls before she'd done something worse—like marrying him.

But after that Gran would have lovingly offered her a shoulder to cry on. Conlon hadn't.

It would take her twenty-four hours, but Isabella would be by her grandmother's bedside until she woke up. And Gran *would* wake up. She had to.

Alone, seven floors above the Hanoi street, Isabella said quietly, 'I'm coming, Gran…' To her sister whom she'd ring shortly, she promised silently, *Nadia, I've got your back.*

She'd find a job at the nearest hospital, visit Gran, be there for Nadia in the last months of her pregnancy. She'd get back to doing what she needed to do. Caring for those who loved and wanted her. Working with babies. She would leave behind Vietnam…this foray into academia… Conlon. Leave behind any silly little girl fantasies that men could be relied on.

She'd learnt that lesson. Oh, yes.

CHAPTER ONE

Three weeks later, Gold Coast, Australia

NORMALLY DR SIMON PURDY, senior consultant paediatrician at Coolangatta Central, wouldn't notice a new nurse in the neonatal intensive care unit.

But today wasn't normal. Because seeing this new nurse hit him like a wrecking ball and he actually staggered. Mayhem exploded in Simon's chest and gut, and he could barely shift his gaze from the stranger across the room as he found his balance.

The unfamiliar sensations had begun when he'd seen her smile as she chatted with a newborn in an open cot—as if the baby could answer.

The tiny patient had done something that had made the nurse's mouth stretch softly until her whole face lit up with mischief.

She was so vibrant—good grief, she hummed with it. Visibly pulsing with life and vitality that made him see, and feel, the depth of his own emotional emptiness.

Now, suddenly and rudely awakened, he remembered he was alive. A man. A broken one. But still a man.

Then all he could think about was his inability to keep those he'd cared for safe. He didn't want to look at that frozen guilt that had been a part of his life for so long. His failure. His culpability that those he'd dared to love were dead.

Thankfully he'd made it to a dimmer corner of the clinical area before he'd been stricken by this strange paralysis and he'd had to force his hand up just to loosen his irritatingly constricting too-tight Tigger tie.

The new nurse, just for a moment, had looked like an angel. Blonde and gentle. Bathing him with healing light.

And then she'd turned side-on, and those curves had not made him think of his lost wife or celestial chastity. She was tall and strong. Like some goddess he had no right to covet. Someone else he would lose if he let himself care. Her thick plait of sun-and-sand-coloured hair swung and danced, with the end of the plait pointing to her backside like a neon arrow, as she floated across the polished floor checking the cots.

'Can I help you, Dr Purdy?'

Simon blinked. At least his eyelids worked again. He swivelled his head—though not his taut body—and looked at Carla, his good friend, and the neonatal nursery's unit manager. The woman who'd nagged him to get on with his life.

She'd spotted him and had her list of patients prepared for him, as usual, in order of urgency. But right now her head was tilted to the side and her eyes twinkled.

'Do you need help?'

He did. But nobody could help him. Where was his usual wall? His defences?

'No.'

The word came out unexpectedly. Just as the woman across the room was unexpected. He blinked again. 'Sorry, Carla. I'm off in another land. Thinking about a patient,' he lied.

Why did he lie? He never lied. Apparently he wasn't very good at it, either.

Carla snorted. 'That's Isabella Hargraves. Very experienced neonatal nurse. Her dad's Professor Piers Hargraves, the neurologist.'

'Head of Neurology at Sydney Central? Chair of Neurology Australia?'

Hopefully she was a socialite, then.

He was dreaming, A quiet, insidious voice inside his head whispered, *But maybe a one-night stand?*

'The same. Isabella's a midwife and neonatal nurse who loves babies. That's what she said when she interviewed. But she's also worked in retrieval, has five scientific papers to her name and has great experience across diverse units. She's moved from Sydney to here to be with her sick grandmother and pregnant sister.'

Simon shook himself.

Loves babies? Good sister? Caring granddaughter?

Despite her stunning looks she was a family

girl. Not for him, then. Danger with a capital D. Nothing to fancy there. He liked surfing alone, working hard and staying too busy with other people's babies to think about having any of his own.

That woman there could break hearts and he was not going there. Damn her. He'd already had more heartbreak than he could deal with. He turned his back on the unit. For some bizarre reason it made him angry with the newcomer.

'Let's see your list, Carla.'

Carla eyed him shrewdly. Handed over the patient list.

She murmured, 'I saw your friend Malachi Madden the other day. He even made a joke—a funny one. Seems having a family suits him.'

Simon raised his brows and side-eyed her without lifting his head.

'And your point?' he asked.

Carla pushed up one shoulder, her mouth kinking with amusement as she winked at him.

'Does there have to be a point, Simon? Could you perhaps think of something other than work? Just for a moment?'

CHAPTER TWO

IT WASN'T UNUSUAL for Isabella Hargraves to feel a stranger's gaze, so she didn't take much notice of the tall man in the corner. Although she had to admit that he wasn't a bad piece of eye candy—despite the scowl.

She'd eased so joyfully back into working with babies in the NICU that it would take more than some random non-admirer to divert her from her tasks.

When the apnoea alarm sounded from Baby Jones she was at his open cot in an instant. Checking the time. Checking the monitor. Watching for breaths as the heartbeat slowed with a brief dip into bradycardia before righting itself as he eventually took a breath.

'Good boy,' she murmured.

She silenced the alarm, and by the time she lifted the chart to record the time and duration of the bradycardia, Carla and the tall man were next to her.

'Isabella.' Carla indicated the man beside her. 'This is Dr Simon Purdy.'

Ah, Dr Purdy… Isabella connected the name with the cot cards. She lifted her head and smiled. 'Nice to meet you, Dr Purdy.'

This man's name sat on the identification cards

of nearly every open-sided cot in the place. Obviously, here stood the favoured paediatrician. She'd heard the staff rave about his thoroughness, dedication and diagnostic abilities since she'd arrived here.

Up close? Oh, my… He was more than just eye candy. Broad-chested and broad-shouldered with tanned, handsome features and a crop of wayward golden hair. He was the full sweetshop. His eyes were the blue of the Coolangatta waves across the road from the hospital, but for some reason his gaze pierced her with surprising harshness. Her smile dimmed. Even his sinful mouth had been pulled into a taut line.

He nodded his blond head briefly—his face all carved cheek bones, patrician nose and strong chin—but his cool eyes swept away from her to the cot.

Obviously, he'd found her lacking in his previously extended perusal. 'Nurse Hargraves.' His voice was deep and dismissive.

Her brows furrowed. *Nurse?*

So, he was doing titles. Everyone else here was on a first-name basis. But he could call her what he wanted. She was actually a doctor of midwifery. She had a PhD. She gave a mental shrug. She could use professional focus against rudeness.

'Self-righting apnoea?' he questioned. Curt and clipped. Cool, even. Barely courteous.

'Yes. Self-stimulation. Sixteen seconds duration. Heart rate dipped to seventy beats per minute.' She handed him the chart.

Baby Jack Jones, his parents having only yesterday decided on his first name, was ten days old and had arrived six weeks before his due date. He lay pink and placid in the cot in front of them.

Jack's heart rate monitor read one hundred and twenty beats per minute—directly at the lower end of the perfectly normal range.

'When was his last feed?'

Although a full tummy often caused a baby's heart rate to drop post-feeding, Dr Purdy's tone seemed taciturn for a man so many had raved about. Still, a chilly tone wasn't Isabella's problem, or even interesting.

She leaned forward and touched the chart, pushing his long, elegant finger aside to lift the top sheet. The feed chart lay underneath the observation chart. But he'd know that. So why ask her the question?

'Thirty minutes ago,' she told him.

'No problems during the feed?'

'No.'

She glanced at Carla, surprised to find a glare in her boss's eyes that was certainly directed at Dr Purdy. Carla's brows were crinkled and her eyes narrowed.

Was he acting out of character? And if so, why?

Did she care?

Nope.

Isabella smiled and moved away from the ward round that she would normally follow with attentiveness. Dr Purdy didn't like her for some reason, though how that could be when they hadn't met before, she didn't know. It was not something that happened often, she realised, giving herself another mental shrug.

She glanced up at the big ward clock. Almost time for Baby Timms to be tube fed.

Cosette Timms was the smallest baby in the unit at the moment, weighing in at seven hundred and thirty grams. She'd been born premature at twenty-nine weeks, thanks to her mum's eclampsia, but had passed the fifteen-hundred-gram mark now.

Isabella would warm expressed breast milk from the fridge and prepare syringes to feed Cosette.

Carla had mentioned that Ellen Timms, Cosette's mum, phoned every morning and evening to check on her daughter.

Isabella had taken the phone call this morning. Mum wasn't coming in. She normally managed the three-hundred-kilometre round trip from the family farm twice a week—even with her other children and her husband's disability after a farm accident. But she couldn't make it today because of a home drama. There was plenty of frozen expressed milk, prepared by Ellen for just such an occasion.

Not at this feed but just before the next one, it would be Cosette's weigh time, and the baby would have to be stripped off and redressed for weighing. Being handled too often tired the premature infants—so it coincided with bath day. Isabella had plans to sending cute bath and weigh-in photos to Ellen from the ward's mobile phone.

Isabella pictured the mum's delight at receiving the pictures as she bustled around the milk room, preparing the feed. She checked the labelled container against the chart, hailed one of the other passing NICU nurses to confirm and countersign the chart, and withdrew the correct amount of milk into the syringe to heat up.

'Isabella?' Carla called out to her.

The nurse who'd co-signed the chart with Isabella reappeared and gestured to the apparatus in her hands.

'Carla said I should take over. She's got another job for you.'

'Oh…' Isabella put the syringes and the bottle of milk down and nodded. 'Okay. Thanks.'

She washed her hands, a small frown crinkling her brows until she let it go. Hopefully, she'd still get to bath Cosette later.

She crossed the room to where Carla stood with Dr Purdy and tilted her head. 'Do you need me, Carla?'

'Yes. I've been called to a managers' meeting and Dr Purdy wants to re-site Jack's IV cannula.

You know how unstable Jack can be, so I'd rather you assisted here for the moment.'

'Of course.' Isabella glanced around until she spotted the trolley they used for procedures and Jack's chart. And anything else she might need.

Dr Purdy glanced at his watch.

Isabella raised her brows at him before saying placidly, 'Give me a moment to set it up, Dr Purdy. Then I'll be with you.'

He seemed to drag his eyes away from his expensive diver's timepiece and nodded. Thankfully, he then turned to the last cot and picked up the chart.

Well, at least he wasn't going to stand there and watch her while she made everything ready. That was a good thing, but Isabella was way past worrying about nervousness with new doctors.

They came in such variety. She'd dated more than a few herself before she fell for Conlon, though most seemed to be obsessed with their own importance.

Probably Freud could have told her why she'd gone for those doctors. Daddy complex. It was a terrible thought.

But now? Hah! No more doctors or lecturers for her. She'd given up the idea of expecting anything from them except self-absorption and egotism.

She knew that was perhaps unfair. But she'd been to so many boring medical fundraising dinners with her father, and playing hostess at her father's house, she'd met many impatient doctors like Simon Purdy.

Most seemed to be in awe of their own intelligence, without observing that Isabella could have run rings around them. Though that didn't matter because she'd chosen midwifery and neonatal nursing.

She liked the hands-on patient care. She didn't want to sit all day in consulting rooms, only being allowed out for surgeries or emergencies—which mostly came during family time if her childhood had been anything to go by.

She wanted continuity of patient care. Being somewhere like here at the NICU, watching tiny newborns struggle, change and finally grow into good health. This was what she wanted to do.

That first rotation through a neonatal nursery had changed her life. She'd found her calling and taken herself to the top of her game as a neonatal intensivist. She'd been asked to join the neonatal emergency retrieval consultancy board, and through that had met neonatologists from all over the world. Which had led to her writing her thesis in Vietnam.

Conlon had jumped on board, seeing an opportunity to advance his own career by sharing the scientific paper she'd spent a year preparing.

She wasn't going there.

Deftly, she completed setting up for the procedure. She had at hand two different types of intravenous fluids, in case Dr Purdy wanted to change the intravenous concentrations. She washed her hands again.

Dr Purdy wasn't obviously looking at her, but she still felt his scrutiny despite that. It was as if he couldn't grasp something he should be able to see.

Well, she had things to do.

'When you're ready, Dr Purdy…'

CHAPTER THREE

SIMON WATCHED NURSE HARGRAVES out of the corner of his eye, refusing to think of her as Isabella. Although, grudgingly, he had to admit it was a beautiful name.

He couldn't help his strange fascination, or being impressed by her. She moved gracefully, efficiently and without hesitation as she gathered supplies and opened them onto the sterile field. Her obvious experience seemed to be at odds with her apparent youth.

Maybe she wasn't as young as she looked—but she was younger than him. And she was full of life and energy. Unlike him. She made him feel old.

As he glanced at her long, graceful neck, his breath caught again, until he had to force his eyes back to the chart that he hadn't even read once.

He wasn't that old. Just sleepwalking through life…until now.

What was it about her?

Dispassionately, you might say her eyes were too big—yet they shone like pools of jungle-green and gold, like a lioness guarding her small cub. Her nose was too straight. No, not straight… refined. It suited her face perfectly. Darn it, he wasn't going to say her mouth was too big…because seriously that mouth was to die for.

Was he sixteen years old?

'When you're ready, Dr Purdy…'

He'd sworn he would never be ready again. He wasn't ready now. He wasn't.

His mouth felt dry—parched, like the sand across the road at the beach. And he swallowed once before he answered, 'Thank you.'

Simon's critical gaze skimmed over the dressing trolley that looked to include anything he could possibly want. Forcibly, he cleared his mind of everything but the task at hand. He lifted Jack's tiny hand and studied the translucent skin and the tiny, thread-like veins beneath.

Simon noticed Nurse Hargraves had the tips of her fingers very gently resting on Jack's foot, as if reassuring him. He'd forgive her the disruption to his world for that.

'Thank you. Everything looks perfect.'

As they worked, she seemed to know what he'd ask for next. They didn't speak and, though they were both unhurried, the procedure was completed smoothly and successfully within minutes.

He frowned at the dexterous and innovative way she wrapped the insertion site.

'That's different. And better than the way I do it. Can you show me again? Please.' He handed her a small splint to mimic a baby's arm and opened another canula packet and held it up to her. 'On this?'

He poked at the facsimile.

'I like the way you've taped it down. Without any strain. And yet so secure. Teach me?'

Simon had forgotten for the moment that he was bizarrely attracted to her. His mind wanted to know how to perform this technique that looked far more comfortable for the infant.

'It's a trick I learned in Vietnam,' she replied.

He watched her fingers while she dipped and circled the cannula, then secured the tape to the imitation arm. Absently he asked, 'When were you in Vietnam?'

'Last month. Helping out in a neonatal unit in Hanoi on an exchange organised by the university in Sydney for a paper I was writing.'

Simon nodded as he began to wrap Jack, who'd fallen asleep. When the baby was secure, Simon tucked him gently back into his open cot, then ensured all the alarms for the monitors were switched back on.

'What's the paper on?' he asked.

'Outcomes in neonatal nurseries in Vietnam, and how to raise Vietnamese community awareness for screening and neonatal care for congenital abnormalities.'

She reeled it off as she worked, cleaning up as fast and efficiently as she'd prepared. She seemed to know where everything was in the unit already as she slipped things they hadn't used back into their correct place. She'd only been here a day. He knew that. He came here every day. Many times. He would have noticed her if she'd been here longer.

He liked her forethought in learning the layout of the unit—she'd ensured that she'd be ready for emergencies. Impressive.

Lots of things about her impressed him.

Stop it.

He murmured, 'I've never been to Hanoi. How was the unit? The staff?'

'The unit's not as high-tech as this one. But the staff are amazing. The aim of my study was to encourage more antenatal attendance with the advantage of picking up potential problems before they happen.'

'Sounds like an interesting study.'

'It was.'

Something in her voice said she wasn't happy with how it had ended.

Then another apnoea alarm began to chime, and she turned and calmly walked across the room to observe and record the event. The alarm stopped.

Simon glanced around the unit. He knew all their patients were stable for the moment. He also knew that he should get to his consulting room for the morning's appointments, but he felt strangely reluctant to leave. Which reminded him: he was supposed to be distancing himself from this woman. Their conversation had pushed her even further under his skin. He needed to stop that. Back away. Fast.

That might have been why was curt as he said, 'I'll be in my office if Carla needs me.'

She lifted her hand but didn't turn around. He guessed he was dismissed. But for some absurd reason he could still see her in his mind.

CHAPTER FOUR

THE FOLLOWING MORNING the sun offered Isabella a pastel bouquet for breakfast—along with a text from Conlon, which she deleted unread.

On the horizon, the guava-pink sky hung with eggshell edges, and where the ocean fell off the edge of the world it turned strawberry around the glow in the east.

'Red sky in the morning,' Isabella murmured. 'Got the warning.'

And it's nothing to do with my new job, the swanky and cranky Dr Simon Purdy, or anything else. Not today. No, siree.

After Hanoi—and the disappointment caused by her ex—being back in Australia with Gran felt right. Her grandmother's condition had been labelled 'stable', but she was no closer to waking.

Isabella had found her sister Nadia to be well, and the promise of Isabella surfing just outside her door made this place feel like an adventure she wanted to live through every day of her life.

Except for Dr Simon Purdy.

Rainbow Bay, so aptly named, had settled into her mind as a sandy paradise. The ocean vista waved and frothed ahead of the break wall of rocks that lined the eastern edge of the beach and greeted each wave.

This is the best place to be, she mentally reassured herself.

No Sydney traffic snarling her up on the way to the beach. No disappointment waiting for her—like Conlon, who was still oblivious to his disloyalty. No daily hurt caused by her father's dismissal because he was far away in Sydney.

Gran's apartment, just a few steps to the beach and one floor from the top, gazed across the bay towards the tall skyscrapers of Surfers Paradise in the distance. The same skyscrapers that right now were blazing windows of blinding gold reflecting the sunrise from across the waves.

The drone of a plane rose above the din of the surf for a moment, until the plane disappeared behind the hill of apartments to her left to land at the hidden airport.

Why on earth hadn't she thought to come to the Gold Coast earlier, instead of working in Sydney? Why hadn't she stayed close to Gran—the most important woman in her life? Because now it might be too late.

She should have had more quality time with Gran. Especially now her widowed sister had bought a tiny courtyard apartment in her grandmother's small block facing the beach. The ground floor apartment seemed perfect for when the baby was born.

Isabella had moved into her grandmother's spare room in a bittersweet temporary arrangement while Gran lay unconscious two kilometres away, in the hospital's critical care unit. Isabella visited every day.

This morning, day two of her new job, she sat on Gran's balcony, watching the ocean and the world awaken. Drinking green tea with jasmine, she studied the water and tried not to think about the irritating Dr Purdy, who'd gone back behind his grim rock façade after the brief period of rapport they'd had while re-siting Jack's cannula.

She just wished she could remove his annoyingly handsome face from her mind, but he lurked and aggravated her like a jagged splinter in her finger. Maybe if she scraped him out and examined him under the light like a wood shaving the annoyance would go away.

Nope. Not going there.

As if to distract her, the currents and swells ebbed and flowed, whispering their secrets, and hidden rocks showed themselves briefly. Peace—at last—seemed to soak into her, like a rock pool into a sea sponge, until her disquiet eased.

As the light grew, she watched the first surfers run to the water. Watched a lithe and powerful man run out to the back of the swells, catch a monster of a wave and ride it like quicksilver skimming the crest.

Nice.

She watched the foamy lines of rips. Looked for the best places away from the rocks and the longest rides into the beach. She worked out where she wanted to take her first surf on Rainbow Bay, tomorrow. Then she rose to get dressed for work.

'So, Gran. Today was my second day at the hospital. I think I'll really enjoy working in the unit here.'

Her grandmother's chest rose and fell.

'Carla, the unit manager, is the best kind of boss. Calm and sensible, with one of those honest faces I really like. You know that she's really *seeing* you.'

Isabella glanced across the sheets to the wrinkled face so dear to her. Gran, who had always *seen* her and Nadia, giving boundless love without coddling them.

But Gran's eyes were shut now. The wrinkled lids hiding the faded green of her irises, probably like Isabella's would in fifty years. Gran's eyes were closed as they had been since the accident, when her head had suffered the blow that had silenced her. But Gran's chest rose and fell in those shallow breaths that Isabella tried to tell herself were good enough. At least she was breathing for herself and not through a machine.

'Anyway... The unit is state-of-the-art. There are babies in there I adore already. There's this little girl—Cosette. Her mum lives an hour and a half away. She runs a farm, but still comes to visit and drop off expressed breast milk three times a week. Her husband was disabled in a farm accident, and she has three other kids. I can't wait to meet her. She sounds like a champion.'

Isabella watched the red electronic trace of her grandmother's heartbeat on the monitor above the bed. Rarely, there was a variation that suggested she might wake. But there were no signs that Gran could even hear her.

Isabella's father—expert neurologist that he was—had reminded Isabella that the longer the oblivion continued the less chance there was that her grandmother would ever wake. So clinical, even when it was his own mother he was talking about. She'd wanted to hit him.

Even more so when he'd said, 'Or if she does wake, she will most likely be in a vegetative state.'

It had been three weeks and three days since the accident and her father had given what scarce hope he ever had, away.

Lately, even Nadia seemed to be accepting that Gran was gone. But Isabella couldn't.

It was Isabella who had begged her father to request that Gran stay here, in the high-dependency unit at the private hospital, which was not quite critical care but still well-watched, for another month before they transferred her to a long-term facility.

Isabella would come and talk to Gran for as long as it took. She knew that the last sense to go in an unconscious body was hearing. She came every day for at least half an hour, either before or after work, depending on the shift, and shared the events of her day.

'There's this paediatrician—Simon Purdy. I loathe him. Don't start me on him. If he wasn't such an excellent neonatologist...'

She frowned at herself.

She *thought* she loathed him.

'Actually, he's too good at intubation and cannulation with tiny babies for me to loathe him. He managed to intubate this twenty-nine-weeker today, in less time than I had to think about it. And he got the cannula in on the first attempt. Pretty incredible. But he's still a pain.'

There—that sounded right.

'But I'm not wasting any more of our time talking about him. I had my first surf this morning.'

Gran had taught her to surf.

'You would have loved this big wave I caught...'

On Thursday Gran's heart rate had risen by ten beats per minute. Isabella checked her observation charts. There was no sign of a temperature, and even her respirations had increased in depth.

Was she getting better? Closer to surfacing? Or was Isabella dreaming?

This was a good sign, wasn't it? Or was it an infection?

'How are you, Gran?' Isabella picked up the

limp, age-spotted hand and lifted it to her cheek. 'Are you okay?'

Gran's hand was cool and dry, so Isabella squeezed her fingers softly and lowered them to the bed as she sat.

'Well, this week flew by, with busy shifts at work. But these daily doses of Simon Purdy are getting harder to take. Remember I said that first day he'd started cold and then got almost civil after Jack's cannula re-siting? Well, since then he's barely said a word to me.'

Her grandmother breathed. In and out.

Isabella sat silently for a bit.

'It's weird… It's as if I can feel his eyes drilling into my back every time I turn around. Like he doesn't want me to catch him looking. But if I turn, he's spinning away. What's with that?'

She frowned at the monitor as she thought about it. And the heart rate rose for a few beats and then fell.

Isabella turned back to her grandmother and looked down at the small hand in hers. 'And of course he's as nice as pie to everyone else in the unit. So why am I getting the silent treatment? What did I do to him?'

She felt her own heart rate speed up as she thought of the unfairness of Simon Purdy's behaviour. Felt her eyes narrow. She'd like to kick him. Which was so unlike her she almost gasped.

Gran's chest rose and fell. The line on the monitor didn't change again. But it was if a thought had wriggled into her brain from the pillow beside her. Almost as if her grandmother had answered.

Isabella said slowly, 'Me being there must be doing something to him. But what?'

Of course she hadn't done anything. But the thought sat there. Hanging. Germinating.

Isabella's brows drew together again. 'Seriously, Gran. The man doesn't seem to have a life outside the unit. He's never impatient to leave or to go home. He was there every morning before I got in this week, and still there for the afternoon shift.'

She'd thought it often enough, and finally she said out loud,

'He reminds me of Dad. Spending his life at work. I pity his poor family.'

She sat back in the chair and thought about that. She could actually imagine a quarter-sized boy, the image of Simon, with the same ocean-blue eyes and full mouth, blond hair and scuffed knees. A little boy waiting for his father to come home. It made her sad for that little boy…

She refocussed. Sad for an imaginary little boy? What was wrong with her?

'Does he even have a wife?' she wondered aloud.

She'd been there a week and she still didn't know. Well, she'd know if she let people tell her. But for some crazy reason she kept holding up her hand when any colleague—and there were a couple who loved to gossip—started to wax lyrical about Simon and his life. She didn't want to know.

Why was that?

Friday dawned with another perfect daybreak in paradise, and Isabella needed the cool water in the bay to wake her after an unsettled night. Her feet slapped rhythmically on the cool sand as she ran towards the surf. Her board lay tucked securely under her arm and her anticipation rose, like the waves out there, as she carried it across the cool pre-dawn beach towards the water.

'Morning,' a chic, elderly woman called out as she passed, lifting her hand as her cavoodle chased seagulls at the edge of the water.

'Best time of the day!' Isabella called back.

The woman, Elsa Green, lived two floors down in the apartment building. She was a friend of her grandmother's.

Isabella's run to the surf slowed, as if a sea fog had rolled over her, as she remembered the cheeky, wise woman her grandmother had been for both her and her sister before that horrible day everything changed. She'd been such a loving set of soft arms when her father had been immersed in work. A rock in their childhood until she'd moved north to Rainbow Bay.

It was tragic. Unfair. But when were accidents ever fair?

She lifted her chin. Catherine Goodwin Hargraves would wake up.

Moving here had been one of Isabella's best ideas. And Nadia selling her ostentatious and heavily mortgaged house to buy the apartment under Gran's was a great move. Meanwhile Isabella could stay and mind Gran's apartment upstairs, so it would be perfect for when she came home.

And Gran *would* come home.

Isabella was already helping Nadia in the last months of pregnancy. Which only bolstered her need to be close to her sister and Gran. Rainbow Bay worked perfectly. Isabella could surf and Nadia could photograph endlessly. And soon there would be a baby—Nadia's baby. And Isabella wouldn't be in her sister's pocket because they had the separate apartments. She might even buy her own apartment in the block if one came on the market.

She just wished Gran was there with them...

The first wave slapped her knee as she jogged deeper into the breaking wash. The water soaked her thighs and waist and she sucked in a breath at the delicious coolness.

Her gaze scanned the distance and she let thoughts of the past and the present fade. She observed about two dozen riders out there with the waves, but she was concentrating on the swells. Rollers that were big enough to give a nice run in towards the beach but with no need to concentrate excessively on avoiding others with her unsettled mind.

It was Simon Purdy who had caused all this twitching and turning through the night. It didn't matter which shift she worked, he turned up at least three times and never seemed to be in hurry to leave.

He took up so much space—and not all of it physical. Though his shoulders and big bronzed arms could block the light, his hands were always gentle and capable.

She could almost see the way his mind zeroed in on their small charges, making him aware of the status of every baby in the unit. She could see it because she did the same.

An ill baby could keep him there for hours. And now, for some illogical reason, he'd apparently decided he needed Isabella as his private assistant for the trickier procedures. Even when she would have preferred not to be called upon because she was doing something she particularly enjoyed.

Especially as he still didn't talk to her.

If he hadn't been so good at what he did she'd have lost patience with him long ago, but she wanted those babies to be well as much as he did.

It was the fact that he talked to everybody else except her that made her seethe. He treated all others with friendliness and respect, while she got the serious looks, the furrowed brows, the unsmiling mouth and gestures rather than words. Hand signals. Head-nods. It wasn't fair. And, if she was honest, it was more than a little annoying.

Yet at other times she caught his glance on her and felt his attention on her back. It was as if he didn't trust her. Which was ridiculous when he'd said himself she was easily the most experienced neonatal nurse in the unit alongside Carla. What was there not to trust?

A wave slapped her in the face—she hadn't seen it coming. And there he was again, intruding on her special time. *Grr...*

Isabella put her head down and paddled, her hands digging into the water, shooting past other surfers as she arrowed through swells and crests and pushed for the back of the sets. She was using up the energy that seemed to be zinging around her body like some electrical conduit of annoyance.

She looked up. There was just the ocean in front of her, all the way to New Zealand, and she finally stopped. As she sat back on her board, legs dangling in the clear blue water, she twisted to face the beach a couple of hundred metres away, then looked back to the far horizon.

She was alone, except for the guy to her left with his back to her, who seemed to be checking out the route to New Zealand as well.

But there wasn't time to think of him. The largest swell she'd seen this morning was rolling towards her and she lifted her feet and pressed her belly and breasts into the board and began to paddle, timing the connection.

Out of the corner of her eye she saw the other surfer shift to do the same. Plenty of room between them. This wave was a monster—one of those walls of water that people didn't notice but came every couple of sets and washed fishermen off rocks. The type of wave that gave surfers the best rush. A wave that reminded her that the sea was royalty and she just its subject.

The power and height of the wave surged swiftly and smoothly and she did the same, springing to her feet and tucking her board on the shelf of water like the bow of a boat. Wind dragged at her hair. Her eyes watched the water shoot below her and around her.

Blue everywhere—above her and beneath her. The sky, the wind… The world was condensed into this ride along the shoulder of a magnificent wall of myriad coloured water.

Her feet danced as she adjusted angle and weight, almost flying as she shot faster and closer to the beach, until the water monster collapsed under her and she slid out at the back and surfaced in a wash of foam and clinging magic.

Isabella lifted her chin, tilted her face to the sky and whooped.

She turned to see if the man at the back of the waves had made it, to share the moment, but he was already paddling away. He must have made it, because he was close, but she had been in a world of her own.

CHAPTER FIVE

SIMON HAD NOTICED the glorious woman before she'd entered the water. Hell, every man out at the back of the waves had noticed her in those bikini bottoms under a short-sleeved surf shirt. Her board sat under her arm as if it was a flimsy paddle-pop stick, rather than a finned, fibreglass weight. Her long, luscious legs bronzed by the sun, glided smoothly as she ate up the distance between the sand and the launch point.

She hadn't been looking his way—her eyes had been fixed on the sets of waves, the wash, the horizon—but he'd been drawn, then, to her face.

His stomach had twisted as if a shark had come up from beneath him and chewed on his intestines.

Not happening. Couldn't be.

His breath had hitched as his chest went tight. It was *her.*

He'd almost fallen off his board—not something he would have lived down with his peers—but he'd stopped himself wobbling in time to absorb the shock. Might as well have been slapped in the nose by a neighbour's board. But his eyes had stayed glued to her.

Isabella Hargraves had run into the waves and launched herself on top of the board and then begun to paddle towards him, squashing her beautiful breasts. Which had meant the taut globes of her tanned buttocks had been there for all to see as her strong, feminine arms arrowed through the swells towards the quieter water.

The force of the biggest wave in the world couldn't have stopped him watching.

Me and all the rest of the guys out there, he'd thought sourly, as he'd glanced around.

Yep. She was poetry in motion. And the last thing he needed to see. Or feel.

But, dammit! This was *his* beach—*his* sanctuary—and now she was here to destroy the peace he'd fought for all week.

Another ghastly thought intruded.

Was he going to bump into her every morning when the surf was up as well as at work?

This was wrong. Already she was taking up too much headspace just by him seeing her in the NICU. He didn't need her glorious backside and her long, lean legs to kick him when he was down.

Since that first day he hadn't been able to ignore her, no matter how hard he'd tried. And he had tried. He'd managed to shore up his defences by barely speaking to her, so that he didn't get any closer, but he couldn't keep his eyes and his thoughts away.

Thankfully, his ridiculous fascination had kept his mouth shut. But, bizarrely, his brain kept going back to that brief rapport they'd had that first day, and how she'd felt like the easiest person in the world to talk to. How much more he'd wanted to know about her... How he'd wanted to lose himself in her fiercely intelligent eyes and revel in the elusive dream he'd vowed would never be his again.

That was when he'd really panicked.

Carla was on his case for giving Isabella the cold shoulder and apparently singling out a staff member she really, really wanted to keep, so he'd agreed yesterday afternoon that he'd try harder to be civil to Nurse Hargraves.

But his whole psyche had screamed *danger* right along with *hot, hot, hot* when he looked at Isabella.

Simon would not let anyone close again. His own mother had died giving birth to him. And he would not put himself out there to risk the grief, the loss and the monumental guilt he still carried from three years ago when he'd lost his wife.

Louise had been his first love, the first woman he'd allowed to get close to him. He'd sworn to protect her and keep her safe.

Probably another guilt trip left over since his seventh birthday, when his father told him that *he'd* been the reason his mother had died. A fact that his older, medically trained self knew was spurious, but it was still so hard to convince the seven-year-old kid inside him.

Then Louise and their son had died. When he

had been absent—working. And despite his best friend—his wife's doctor—telling him that nothing would have changed the outcome, Louise's death had damaged him. Adding to the loathing his father had heaped on him in the dark times of his childhood.

In short, he was not going down the route of attraction, falling in love, planning a life together and then losing the one he'd pinned his future on ever again. *Ever.*

Never.

No matter how glorious Isabella Hargraves was. No matter how much poetry in motion he saw in her.

He just wasn't sure how he was going to stop himself.

CHAPTER SIX

WHEN ISABELLA WALKED into the unit later that morning, the ferocious glower she received from Simon Purdy could have shrivelled her on the spot.

She froze. Stared. Glared back at him.

The calmness and tranquillity from her amazing surf this morning seemed to trickle away like seawater down her back, leaving her cold and chilled. And then red-hot with fury. She was *so* over this.

Isabella marched across the unit. Stopped in front of him and asked very quietly, so nobody else could hear, and very clearly, so he would understand, 'What is your problem?'

'You,' he replied.

His blue eyes were stone-hard and his mouth was a thin line.

She narrowed her eyes at him. It was a measure of the build-up of tension over the last week that she allowed her hands to come up to her hips.

'What have I done?' she shot back. 'Or did you just get out on the wrong side of the bed? *Again*.'

Before he could answer, Carla glided up and stepped between them. 'What's going on?' she asked them both, but she was looking at Simon.

Isabella said quietly, and with impeccable calm,

'I don't care if Dr Purdy is the best paediatrician this side of the equator. I expect to be treated with the respect I deserve and the politeness he so easily gives to everyone else in the unit.'

Carla nodded. 'Fair call, Isabella. Simon…?'

Isabella's and Simon's eyes were still locked—neither had looked at the unit manager. Isabella held his gaze—his hard and blue, hers determined not to give in—until he flinched.

She heard his breath heave out and for some strange, stupid reason she actually felt sorry for him.

What the...?

'You're right,' Simon said.

He lifted his chin. Straightened his shoulders. Stared at the wall past her head.

'I apologise, Isabella. Something happened this morning that I shouldn't have brought to work.'

His gaze drifted briefly to Isabella's face. She saw the briefest flicker of searing pain there until he looked away to Carla.

'I'll do better.'

Then he walked out of the unit, leaving Isabella staring after him, still not understanding why she wasn't angry any more and confused as to why on earth she was wishing she hadn't said anything.

Carla must have read her expression. Or else she was prescient.

'It needed saying. And he wasn't listening to

me,' Carla said as she patted Isabella's arm. 'He knows he wasn't being fair.'

'Hi, Gran. How are you today?'

As Isabella leaned over and kissed her grandmother's soft cheek she inhaled the faint, sweet rose scent. Gran still smelled the same as she had for as long as Isabella could remember and the fragrance always made her feel hope that her grandmother would wake up.

That was why Isabella replenished Gran's favourite soap when it shrank, and why the nurses promised to continue to use it during her care.

Isabella sat down. 'Work was fine…'

Gran's chest rose and fell.

'Although this morning, when he came in, Simon Purdy was in a foul mood.' Isabella scoffed. 'He actually glared at me as if I'd done something wrong. So I confronted him. That's not like me, I know, but I was so over the dirty looks. He did apologise. But he looked strange…'

She shook her head.

'I still have no idea what his beef is, and if he wasn't one of the best neonatologists I've ever seen I'd have made a formal complaint. Still, maybe he'll be better now.'

She listened to herself. Gran did not need to hear this.

She blew out a breath. 'Luckily, I had such a great surf before work. So it was like water off a seagull's back. You would have loved this huge wave I caught. It was so good…'

It had been an amazing start to the day.

And then that man… Her mind drifted back to Simon Purdy. It was disconcerting. She'd never had someone take an instant dislike to her before. And then there'd been that look of agony she'd seen.

Gran didn't need to know about that, either. But she felt agitated at the thought of him, and grimaced.

Isabella leaned forward and opened the drawer beside the bed. Her fingers found the tube of rose-scented hand lotion and she reached to pick up her grandmother's hand. She squeezed the tube and gently swirled the lotion onto the papery skin of Gran's hands.

Isabella did this often—sat and gently massaged the long, thin fingers of Gran's hands with the lotion while she talked. As always, a sense of peace settled over her.

'Anyway… Nadia's been getting headaches. I don't think it's pregnancy-related, but her next antenatal appointment isn't until next Wednesday. Hopefully she's going as an outpatient today to get checked, as I suggested, but you know what she's like. Stubborn.'

As Gran breathed in and out her heart rate did that little rise and fall thing again, but Isabella was used to it now.

'You always said we were both stubborn, but I think Nadia's more obstinate than me. I'll find out whether she went when I get home.'

Home. To Gran's apartment without Gran. It was getting harder and harder to imagine her grandmother ever being there when she came home from work. She hated that and hoped she wasn't losing faith like everyone else.

No. She wouldn't. She'd use some of her own stubbornness to stay positive.

'Your flat's looking fine. I haven't killed all your plants.'

Yet, she thought ruefully. Most were drooping, and she didn't know if she was giving them too much water or not enough.

Or maybe they needed more sunlight?

'I mentioned my concerns to Mrs Green…'

Isabella thought about that, and a smile tugged at her mouth.

'So cool that her name is Green and she's good with plants.'

She waited for her grandmother to smile, but of course she didn't.

She shook her head at herself.

'Mrs Green said she'd use her spare key and come up and water the plants on the veranda every other day, when she knows I'm out. She always asks about you. I keep telling her you'll be home soon.'

Gran continued to breathe. In and out.

The monitor continued to trace her heart rate.

By the time Isabella parked her car under the apartments it was nearing four-thirty. Instead of pressing for the lift she climbed the stairs, turned left, and knocked on her sister's door.

When there was no answer, she knocked again. And again. Until she heard Nadia's voice inside. Faintly.

'I'm coming… All right… Give me a minute.'

A cold flicker of worry ignited in Isabella's chest at the dull timbre of Nadia's voice. But at least the shuffling noises were coming closer, and finally the door opened.

Her sister leaned against the door frame like a droopy sunflower, with her yellow hair falling over her face and her long neck bent as if she could barely hold the weight of her head up. Let alone the big belly out front.

'Isabella. It's you.'

Who else would it be?

Isabella pushed the door open and gently turned her sister, nudging her back into the lounge room and into a chair. 'You look terrible.'

'Gee. Thanks, Sis.' Nadia's voice trailed away listlessly.

'Did you go and get checked out today at the hospital?'

'Didn't have the energy.'

'How's your headache?'

'There all the time. All over my head. It's weird…' Nadia lifted a tired hand to rub her scalp.

Isabella peered down and examined her sister's ankles. No, they didn't look swollen. But oedema could happen quickly.

'Are you going to the toilet as much as you normally do?'

Nadia sighed. 'Probably not. But then I'm not drinking or eating either, so there's nothing to pass. I'm a bit sick in my stomach.' She rubbed her abdomen under her breast. 'Probably picked up a bug from somewhere.'

All nebulous symptoms, but worrying. 'I want to take you in and get you checked out in Maternity.'

Nadia shook her head—gingerly. 'Not now. I've just taken two headache tablets. I'm going to go and lie down.' She closed her eyes, as if the light was too bright. 'I was lying down when you knocked.'

'I don't like the look of you… Really. Something's not right.'

Her sister made an effort to sit straighter in the chair. Forced her eyes wider. 'You're a worry-wart. How about I have my sleep, then you come and see me in a couple of hours? Use your key so I don't have to get up. If I'm still no good, I'll go then.'

'I'd be happier if you went now…'

Nadia waved her away. 'But it's not about *you* being happy, is it?'

Time for the big guns.

Isabella's instincts were screaming.

'No. It's about keeping your baby safe,' Isabella said quietly. Her voice was firm and she watched her words finally sink in.

Understanding flooded Nadia's face. And then her green eyes widened in fear. 'Yes. It's about the baby. I'll go now.'

Half an hour after they arrived at the hospital Nadia began to see flashes of light in front of her eyes, and then she started to seize uncontrollably.

Suddenly the clinic was full of people and Isabella retreated to the back of the room. She gave thanks for the hospital policy of one support person being allowed to stay at all times where possible.

Then a tall, dark-haired doctor suddenly strode in and organised everyone in seconds, giving quiet orders that were instantly obeyed.

Isabella's terror receded as Nadia's hypertensive crisis was brought swiftly under control and a care plan commenced.

The new doctor turned to her and introduced himself. 'I'm Malachi Madden, the consultant obstetrician on call today. You're Nadia's sister? And a midwife?'

'Yes.'

'Excellent. So, Nadia has eclampsia—you'll know what I'm talking about. We'll keep her in under one-on-one observation for the next twenty-four hours. If she settles on the medication, we'll see how long we can prolong the pregnancy. Thirty-two weeks is not a great stage for birth, but sometimes it's necessary. We'll start steroids now, to help mature the baby's lungs, with the probability of delivery in the next forty-eight hours.'

His manner was brisk and blunt—which she appreciated—and decisive.

He went on, 'With eclampsia, there's really not much benefit to prolonging the pregnancy, because the environment becomes dangerous for the mother and is no longer optimal for the foetus.'

'I understand. I work in neonatal intensive care.'

'Do you? That's handy.' He smiled at her and, unexpectedly, his smile was sweet and sincere. 'My wife and I have one-year-old twins, and I know babies do give you interesting moments. Your sister will be glad of your advice.'

CHAPTER SEVEN

AT FIVE-THIRTY THE next morning Simon's phone buzzed. He rolled out of bed to sit up and answer the call.

Years ago, as an exhausted med student, he'd learned not to lie down and take phone calls. Though he knew at this time of day he wouldn't fall asleep, because the sun would be up soon and he'd be planning on hitting the beach.

In five out of the last six days he'd been called out before sunrise and had had to go to the hospital instead of enjoying an early-morning surf.

The only day he had made it, his longed-for peace had been slapped for six by a blonde bombshell in tiny bikini bottoms.

He glanced at the caller ID. His registrar. Not surprising. Henry was the most likely person to ring him at an ungodly hour, though he only phoned when he needed advice or help.

'Morning, Simon.' Henry's cheerful voice came down the line. 'Got a new prem. Thirty-two weeks. Female. Two thousand grams. Born an hour ago due to maternal eclampsia and requiring CPAP at the moment, plus a cannula that's proving tricky, but otherwise she's stable.'

'Nothing you can't handle. So what's the problem?' Simon didn't believe in babying his registrars. Because they were the next generation and one day, unimaginable as it was at this moment, he would retire.

'I've had two goes at inserting the line without success, and the baby's auntie said I had to get you.'

Simon's brow furrowed. 'Come again?'

He couldn't think of any of his friends due to have a baby soon. Though it sometimes happened with hospital staff. People recommended him for their grandchildren or asked him to be in charge of sick nieces and nephews. And he always agreed. There had to be some perks for these staff who cared so diligently for others. But those requests usually came when he was on duty. At handover or in normal working hours.

'She said I'm not allowed to try the cannula again.'

Simon mentally shrugged. He was awake anyway. 'Who's the auntie?'

His registrar lowered his voice. 'That new neonatal intensivist… Isabella Hargraves. She said if the kid wasn't her niece she'd put the line in herself.'

Any lingering drowsiness in Simon's mind disappeared like mist in the sun and he remembered that first day, with Carla telling him Isabella had moved here to be with her grandmother and pregnant sister.

'Ahh. Her sister. I'm coming.'

* * *

The first person Simon saw when he entered the unit was Isabella, and his gaze stuck on her like a seagull spotting a lone potato chip. He forced himself to look away as he washed his hands at the sink. Her hair had been pulled back in a blonde ponytail, she wore no make-up, and yet she still looked as if she'd stepped out of a fashion magazine. It was the way she held herself as much as what she wore.

Hell, she looked like a model even when she was in scrubs.

His gaze shifted to the cot she stood beside, and he saw the small bare limbs under the heat lamp, and the monitors and paraphernalia of a prem baby in their care. He inclined his head towards Henry and the night shift nurse as he crossed the room to them.

'Thank you for coming,' Isabella said, her voice softly hesitant.

He wasn't surprised to see uncertainty in her eyes, as if she was not sure of her reception. Yesterday had been a day of fireworks, and they'd been careful to avoid each other since her accusations and his apology.

But it wasn't as if he would ever have declined the request. He realised he hadn't been particularly friendly, but…

'Of course I'd come.'

There was no missing her relief. Though it was

a surprise that she'd want him looking after her niece. And even more personally noteworthy that he found he didn't want anyone else doing it, either.

'Thank you for trusting me.'

He turned to Henry.

'Run me through the history.'

Henry did, and when he was finished Simon nodded. Then another thought intruded.

He looked at Isabella. 'Where's your sister? Is she okay?'

The beautiful woman in front of him sagged a little, and he wanted to put out a hand in sympathy. Badly. But his sense of self-preservation wouldn't let him.

'Nadia's still in Recovery. She had a caesarean section after escalating eclampsia. But she should improve soon, with the end of the pregnancy.'

He could see the concern in the creases of her brow. It must be a big worry for her to carry, and he wanted to ease that burden. He felt the urge to reassure her. Comfort her. Dammit, he wanted to help her in any way he could.

'I'm sorry to hear she's unwell. Who's her obstetrician?'

'Malachi Madden.'

She searched his face for reassurance, and he felt the consolation of being able to give it freely. Relief expanded inside him. His long-time friend was the best.

'Ahh. Great. Excellent choice. He's sharp. He'll look after her.'

'And you'll look after Kate?' she asked.

He could see she'd recovered her usual calm façade, as if he had already helped with his endorsement of Malachi.

'I will,' he told her. 'Absolutely.'

Simon was soon feeling along the edges of the tiny baby's body, skimming the abdomen and watching the equal rising of both lungs.

'Her mum had called her Kate? Great name.'

'Named after my grandmother—Catherine.'

He looked up and saw her gaze had clouded again.

'Gran's not well either.'

He nodded. Said sincerely, 'I'm sorry to hear that.'

Then he shifted his gaze down again. 'Let's have a listen to this little lady.' He raised a brow at Henry. 'You go. I'll stay.'

'Thanks, boss. Been a long night.'

The young man lifted one finger to his forehead in a salute to Simon and tipped an imaginary hat to Isabella. He was grinning as he strode away.

Simon positioned the buds of his stethoscope in his ears and examined his new patient.

He said quietly to the night shift nurse waiting, 'Do we know how the placenta looked? Was it failing? Were all vessels present?'

'The theatre notes haven't arrived, yet.' The nurse was young, nervous, and kept darting glances between Simon and Isabella. 'I'll let you know when they come through.'

'Maybe give them a ring now?' Simon suggested mildly, but the nurse got the message and took off.

He looked at 'Auntie Isabella'. The thought made him want to smile, but there was nothing funny about what she was going through.

'Is there any history of pre-eclampsia with your sister?' he asked.

'No.'

She shook her head and her ponytail flopped over her shoulder. He could see more clearly that she looked tired and a little strung out. Not surprising. And no thanks to him.

In a flash of insight, he regretted the barriers he'd been putting up since he first saw her. She was new to town. She needed kindness, not his prickly defences, and she had a lot going on in her life. He hadn't realised how much. He'd been an arrogant idiot, only thinking about himself and his own insecurities. His own demons. Which wasn't like him.

So why was that? Why act so much out of character? And why had he targeted someone he knew didn't deserve it?

He was afraid he knew why. Fear. Of himself.

For himself. And, riding on the back of that, fear for her if she relied on him.

He had a sudden urge to reach out and touch her shoulder…apologise. Hell, he wanted to pull her into his arms and give her a hug. Of course he couldn't do anything so stupid. But he could breathe in the scent of her. Could watch the expressions cross her face as she looked at Kate.

Thankfully, her eyes were fixed on her niece, not on him.

'When I got home yesterday afternoon Nadia was complaining of a headache,' she explained. 'She looked so unwell I dragged her into Maternity. She started seizures half an hour after we arrived.'

Close call. And scary. She had to be imagining other scenarios.

'Lucky you did what you did.' His voice was soft. He understood the fear of others. He'd been there in the worst way. 'That's nasty. Dangerous for both Mum and baby.'

She started, as if surprised. For a horrid moment he thought she was going to cry. And then she lifted her chin.

'Yes.'

He dragged his eyes from her face, glanced towards the desk, but the young nurse was still on the phone.

'She's in the best place now. Let's have a look at this cannula…'

'Want me to help?'

Isabella had already begun to douse her hands with the cleanser clipped to the sides of all the cots.

Of course he wanted her help. She was the best to work with. But it wasn't fair when it was her own niece.

'You're okay with that?' he asked.

'As long as you don't mind that I called you in.'

He did smile at that. 'No. Never. Though Henry probably would've got the cannula in on the third go.'

'I wasn't willing to risk his next attempt.' She narrowed her eyes. 'Send him to me next week and I'll adjust his technique.'

'I'll do that.'

Simon laughed. Something he hadn't done for a while, except maybe with his friend Malachi and his wife, Lisandra. Henry did tend to rush when he was nervous. Isabella might have made him nervous. Hell, she made *him* nervous—but for a different reason.

That thought sobered him.

'If Kate was my niece, I probably wouldn't have let him try again, either.'

'Yes… Thank you for coming.'

'You're welcome. She looks good, Isabella.'

Suddenly it was easy to talk to her. Like back in the beginning, before he'd put up his great wall. It was something he'd been avoiding thinking about like the plague, because that one time he'd listened, he'd been drawn to her so strongly. He'd backed away in an absolute wild panic, and hadn't wanted to repeat the experience. It hurt too much to care for people and then lose them. So, he'd vowed to keep that wall way up during work—to make it unlikely he'd do anything stupid.

Anyway, she was experienced enough to know what he wanted during procedures without him having to use words. All it took was a lift of his brow and she knew what he wanted. Which made it easier. And harder.

Aside from that, the more he discreetly watched and listened to her, the more he suspected she might be one of the smartest people he'd met.

But now she was a concerned relative. And he talked to her because it was part of his job. She needed to hear what was going on. He passionately believed in not holding back information from those who had the right to be told.

'She's got a heart murmur. Did you hear that?' he asked her.

Isabella had a stethoscope around her neck, and he assumed she'd have listened to her niece's chest.

'I did. Sounds like a PDA. Hopefully, because she's prem, her patent ductus will close as she grows.'

'My thought too.'

Ha! He known she'd pick that up.

'And we both know that children born after twenty-eight weeks of pregnancy, and with a weight like this little lady, have a big chance of having no long-term problems.'

'We know eight out of ten do,' Isabella corrected him.

He smiled to himself, and didn't look at her as he studied the lack of creases on Baby Kate's feet and the cartilage growth of her ears.

'But she's a good weight for thirty-two weeks, so the pre-eclampsia hasn't been a long-term issue she'll have to recover from.'

Her shoulders rose and fell in a sigh. 'When it's your own sister's baby, she looks more tiny and delicate than everyone else's baby. I'm used to seeing babies without toenails and hair, and she has both, but she's so fragile. What do you think of her breathing?'

'I think she's doing well for the day she's had.'

'I know. Don't tell me.' She waved her hand at him, apparently aware he'd been about to say something reassuring. 'Albert Einstein was born two months premature and look at what he achieved.'

She smiled, and he couldn't help smiling back. He'd bet she'd heard that so many times. They'd dined on that story in med school, and he suspected midwives did too.

'Exactly. We'll get her started on some broad-spectrum antibiotics. Do you know if Nadia's going to breastfeed?'

He saw Isabella was looking better for their conversation. More herself. Not so shattered.

'She intends to.'

'Great. She'll have you to help her.'

CHAPTER EIGHT

SIMON PURDY WAS being nice to her, and now she felt like crying. Felt like burying her nose in his big, beautiful chest and sobbing. Of course it was just emotional overload from the last twelve hours. Her sister and niece could have died—highly unlikely in the modern day—but the risk had been there.

And then Isabella had demanded they get Simon. She didn't know how it had happened, and she wasn't normally a pushy person, but she'd stood there watching his registrar's second attempt at placing the cannula and known he wouldn't get it.

She needed Simon on board for her niece. She didn't care if she was being demanding. Didn't care if Simon hated her guts. He was the best. This was all about Nadia's baby and Nadia couldn't be there. Isabella was. And she would be Kate's champion until her mother recovered.

And so here they were. Back to working on a baby together—although she was pretending it wasn't her flesh and blood lying there.

Her hands moved confidently, with muscle memory, as she assembled fresh equipment and Simon prepared Kate's tiny arm for another attempt at the cannula insertion.

He'd come when she'd asked, she thought. So fast. He must live as close as she did. And Henry, the registrar, hadn't been offended, which was a good thing for future professional relationships. Although, even if he had been miffed she would still have demanded Simon.

All these thoughts played in her mind as she watched his long, slender, yet strong hands. Piano player's hands…calm, capable, hands, she thought, her eyes glued to them as they very gently tilted Kate's skin this way and that to catch the light and expose the minuscule thread of veins below the skin.

'One there,' he said, and she peered with him. She inhaled his man scent and felt her pulse jump and her heated skin react to his nearness.

She ignored the sensations. She didn't want to think about them. She returned her mind to Kate, and allowed the relief of seeing Simon's skills to flow over her.

The vein was faint, but clear to see. Henry hadn't seen that one. The tension in her shoulders and neck released. The responsibility had shifted to the man beside her.

Simon Purdy had this all under control. She could relax.

He was here and—surprise, surprise—finally treating her the same way he treated the other staff.

She thought about that. No. Actually, he was treating her as if she was the relative of one of his patients. With reassurance and an unspoken promise to do his best. And yet there was professional appreciation for her as well. She'd seen a glimmer of it before, when they were working together, but it was a little hard to feel appreciated if the person you worked with didn't speak to you.

If her niece wasn't so fragile she'd be thinking all her Christmases had come at once. But for the moment she just wanted to see this cannula in and working.

Within seconds the procedure had been completed successfully and their eyes briefly met in relief. Held for a couple of seconds longer than necessary.

She taped the tiny tube down while Simon held it still. Then they both stood back as the machine began to count the slow drops of fluid running into Kate's arm.

All tension her released and relief washed over her. 'Thank you.'

He smiled at her. His teeth white, his mouth curved and that beautiful, strangely sexy nose of his pointed her way.

'You're very welcome. As always, you're a great right hand.'

'As always, huh?' She tilted her head at him and

raised her brows. Her voice just a little mocking. 'Can't say I've felt that appreciation much over the last week.'

Good grief. Not now. She closed her lips.

Not when he was doing her and Kate a favour.

But he had the grace to look away. 'Some personal stuff,' he murmured. 'Not your fault. But, yes, you copped some of the fall-out. I apologise again for that. My behaviour hasn't been fair.'

That made her blink. She had not expected a confession and another comprehensive expression of regret.

Off balance, she said quietly, 'Why were you so foul yesterday when I came in?'

Lord, it was as if her filters had been lost sometime in the long night.

It was her turn to look away. 'Sorry. Ignore that. It's been an emotional twelve hours.'

His whole body went rigid. His mouth pursed. And then he sighed. Shook his head and turned his gaze to her. He studied her face and then shook his head again. His expression was resigned… even slightly amused.

'Would you like to go for breakfast after this? I know a place that opens early. I can explain.'

And that was another thing she had not expected him to say.

She glanced at the clock. Twenty minutes until

the day staff began to arrive. She was on the afternoon shift today, and she had to sleep. But…

'I guess I need to eat. I've drunk lots of coffee. But no food since lunch yesterday.'

'We'll wait to hand over to Carla…get the morning staff here first, if that's okay with you?'

'Of course. Actually, I'd prefer that.'

'Thought you might.'

He smiled, and she felt that ridiculous urge to cry again.

She didn't think he would notice, but he said softly, so nobody else could hear, 'You'd be eligible for compassionate leave, you know. Next of kin. You should take a day or two, get some sleep, come and go to see Kate and your sister without having to concentrate on your patients.'

That did sound like heaven, and she was so tempted—but she was new here, and couldn't let Carla down. The unit had already been busy before Kate, and a new premmie would stretch their limits.

'I think they'll need more staff…not less.'

'I thought you might say that too.' His blue eyes were too kind. 'We'll see.'

He walked away a few steps, picked up a chair and placed it gently beside Kate's cot. 'Sit here, watch your niece and enjoy her. She's stable, if early in her adventures. I'll do a quick round to check everyone else while we wait.'

So she sat. In the chair he brought for her. And the overwhelming facts finally sank in. She was an auntie. Nadia was safe. And Simon had come to care for Kate.

They'd walked to breakfast. They went to the coffee shop that sat perched above Rainbow Bay, with its high stools and tall benches under red umbrellas, all facing the waves. Jars of pretty purple-blue knives and forks sat in the middle of the tables. Very beachy…

Simon had said he lived too close to the hospital to drive—it was only a block—so he didn't take his car to work. She said she didn't either.

Isabella hadn't realised there was a place so near to where she lived that was open this early. She studied the menu briefly—*yum*—and put it back down. Her stomach rumbled.

The waitress, a young woman with a dozen piercings and her hair shaved so close to her head she was almost bald, grinned at Simon. 'Yo, Doc. The usual?' She patted her pocket and pulled out a pen and notebook.

'Yes. Thanks, Lulu.'

He turned to face her. That lovely, debonair nose of his—which for some reason she liked too much—was suddenly too close to hers and his face, too handsome, was filling her vision.

'You ready to order?'

Order. Right. Stop looking at the pretty man.

'Smashed avocado and eggs, thanks. Plus, your rainbow juice. No coffee. I need to sleep soon.'

'On the way,' Lulu said, and winked at Simon.

He was obviously a regular patron.

'I think the waitress likes you.'

'Lulu's the proprietor. I looked after her twins when they were born. Twin-to-twin transfusion, and the smallest one struggled a bit at first. They're both at preschool now and doing well.'

'No wonder you're a favourite. A story around every corner. Or around every cafe.' She waved her arm towards the other stools. 'Great to know this is here, though. Thanks.'

He lounged in his chair, relaxed, soaking in the sun and the admiration of passers-by like a darned rock star. Not looking as if he'd been dragged from his bed by her. Drat the man. No doubt she looked as if she'd been raking her hair and sleeping in her clothes for the whole night.

'Despite how I look now, I do like to get up early,' she said.

'Me too,' he said, with an odd tone in his voice. 'I've been surfing here for the last three years. It's where I find my peace.'

There was a definite note of pique there. Plus, a strange twist to his beautiful mouth. And why she was noticing all these masculine attributes she did not know.

That was the last thing she needed to do. She needed to eat and go to bed. And put the intriguing Simon Purdy, currently being so pleasant to her, out of her mind. Another workaholic she was drawn to. What was wrong with her?

Then his actual words sank in.

She turned to face him. 'You surf?'

'Mm-hmm,' he said, very dryly.

She crinkled her brows at him. Now that she thought about it, he did have more of a laid-back, world-class surfer look than a rock star gleam, with his blond hair slightly ruffled and his skin tanned bronze. The way his azure-blue eyes crinkled at the corners could be from watching hundreds of promising ocean swells roll his way.

And suddenly she knew.

'You were out at the back of the swells when I was there yesterday.' She should have recognised those shoulders. That hair. 'And later that was you paddling away after that amazing wave.'

'It was.'

She frowned. 'I've been surfing every morning this week. I haven't seen you…'

Then she remembered that first surfer she'd watched, and suspected that had been him as well. How could she have missed him? She couldn't believe she hadn't recognised him yesterday. She guessed on a surfboard was not a place she'd expected to see him. But surely, she hadn't missed him day after day, every morning?

'I've had a run of early call-outs that have impacted on my surf time this week.' He breathed in slowly and let it out. 'Since my wife died, and since I moved to the beach…' He lifted his shoulders, and then his chin. 'The waves and work. That's where I find my peace.'

'You lost your wife?'

Heck. That explained a lot. He was broken. He had a right to be moody.

'I'm sorry for your loss.'

'Three years ago. Louise and our baby both died. Amniotic fluid embolism.'

Disasterous. That happened when amniotic fluid crossed the placenta into the mother's bloodstream. How awful for all of them.

He was looking at her as if he didn't believe her. 'You didn't know? Hospital staff usually make sure everyone knows everything.'

She shook her head. 'I make an effort not to engage. I come from a high-profile family and I dislike gossip.'

'Yes. Carla told me about your father on your first day.' His mouth quirked. 'Apparently, I do listen to gossip. She could see you had made an impact on me.'

She had made an impact on him? When? How?

But he didn't add to the statement. Maybe she had heard him wrong.

Something else bothered her. 'You said you'd tell me what happened yesterday. Why did I get the super-snarly Dr Purdy?'

He rubbed his chin with his knuckles, and looked relieved when their drinks arrived.

Lulu stood for a minute, examining Simon's face. 'Haven't seen you for a while…'

'We've been busy in the NICU. This is Isabella. She's one of those hotshot neonatal nurses—like the ones who came in the helicopter to scoop up Lily when she was transferred.'

Lulu looked impressed and Isabella felt the heat in her cheeks. He'd known that about her, too?

'Cool.' Lulu grinned, and the tiny diamond in her tooth glinted. 'You people are amazing. I hope we see you again another day.'

Isabella smiled back, even if it was a tired smile. She could feel herself wilting.

'You will. I live around here. Or my grandmother did…' *Not did.* 'Does. She *does.* She's in hospital at the moment.'

Why had she started this? She was too tired to be sensible.

'Anyway, thanks…'

Lulu nodded and went off to answer the bell at the kitchen window. It looked as if their food was ready.

Lulu arrived back with their plates just as Simon asked, 'What's wrong with your grandmother?'

His concern warmed Isabella more than it should have, but still she felt the tug of old grief and shock. 'She was knocked over by a hit-and-run driver a month ago. She's still unconscious.'

Simon closed his eyes briefly and muttered, 'I've been stupid…' He shook his head. 'Mrs Hargraves…' He turned his shoulders and pointed to where her grandmother's apartment block was just visible through the trees. 'You're living in her flat?'

'Yes. And my sister bought one in the same block.'

He said something she couldn't quite hear, but it sounded possibly like *Fate is conspiring.*

'Sorry?'

'Nothing.' He lifted his hands and said to the sky, 'Should I just bow to the inevitable? That I'm going to see you everywhere I go?'

Isabella stifled a yawn. 'You're being annoying.'

He tilted his head as if he changed his mind about what he was going to say and gestured for her to eat. 'I'm guessing you've been up for twenty-four hours. You need a sleep.'

He still hadn't told her what his problem had been yesterday, but at that point she just didn't care. She'd got to the stage when she was almost too tired to eat, but she'd better—she'd need some energy to get home.

CHAPTER NINE

SIMON FINISHED HIS breakfast and sipped his coffee while his companion finished hers. Really, there was nothing he could do except make sure Isabella made it to her apartment.

He might as well tell her he lived upstairs, even if she was too tired to comprehend, because it would be stupid to put her into the lift and not get in after her.

Lulu brought the bill and he paid it. Isabella didn't notice as she stared unfocussed into the distance.

Yep, she'd crashed.

'Come on, sleepyhead, I'll walk you home. Can't have you falling asleep in a bus shelter.'

'I will not fall asleep in a bus shelter,' she said with just a little fuzzy haughtiness that he found surprisingly cute. She gathered her bag and slung it over her shoulder. Then she turned back and said, 'Thanks, Lulu. That was wonderful.'

He thought it sweet that she'd appreciated the service. They walked side by side along the path towards the square apartment building that soon loomed over them.

He couldn't believe he hadn't run into her in the lift. But then, he had been keeping odd hours lately. Pretty funny that he'd spent most days with her at work, though, and yet they hadn't realised they shared an address.

As they reached the ground floor entrance she fumbled in her bag and he touched her shoulder. 'I've got it.' He pulled out his keys from his pocket, opened the door, and gestured for her to go in front of him.

She frowned. 'Why have you got a key to this building?'

'Not that sleepy, then?' he said, amused by her suspicion.

She tilted her head back, stared at him with narrowed eyes. He noticed her gaze had lost its dozy inattention.

'I live on the eighth floor,' he said succinctly.

Her eyes widened. 'You're kidding me?'

'I was surprised, too, when I worked it out at the café.'

'So you know my grandmother?'

Her eyes were an incredible shade of green with gold flecks. The world shifted as he stared. His gaze drifted to her mouth, where the words had come from. So soft. Tempting. He could just kiss… And then he woke up. Hot. Bothered. Mentally smacking himself.

She said, 'Hello…?'

Simon stepped back to make more space between them.

Oh, whoa, lost it there for a second.

What the heck had happened?

He'd known this was a bad idea.

He reorganised his thoughts and played back the conversation. 'Yes. Mrs Hargraves? I've met her many times in the lift. She's a lovely lady. I was very sorry to hear about her accident.' He pressed the lift call button and stood back with her to wait.

'She's still unconscious,' Isabella said, in a normal voice.

Maybe she hadn't noticed he'd almost kissed her, he thought. Hoped.

He had almost...what?

'I see her every day, depending on my shift. I'm still praying...' Her voice trailed off.

This was not about him. This was about her world and he had no idea about it.

'You've had a tough month,' he said.

'You have no idea,' she said, as if she'd read his thoughts.

There was just a touch of bitterness that seemed very unlike her, and he wondered what else could have gone wrong for her.

He knew about ghastly times. Things had gone horribly wrong for him.

'Where there's life there's hope,' he said. A trite saying that tasted bitter in his mouth.

During his ghastly time he hadn't even had that—hope. His wife and child had both been gone within minutes. When he wasn't there. No hope. But he was finding a little more distance from the shock as the years passed. And even more since he'd met Isabella.

What?

He took another step back as the lift doors opened. He was suddenly very conscious of how small the lift was, and how close they'd be. Maybe he should dash back to the hospital to check on Kate?

'Get in. I won't bite,' she said, and thc super-confident woman he'd first met was back in placc.

He felt his cheeks warm. He hadn't blushed since high school. But he stepped in and the doors closed.

She pushed buttons seven and eight. 'You never told me what happened yesterday.' Her eyes widened. 'And I didn't pay for breakfast.'

'I settled the bill. You were half asleep. You can pay next time.'

Next time? Was there going to be a next time? Heaven help him.

The lift stopped and he put his hand across the doors to prevent them closing prematurely on her.

'Phone me directly if you're ever worried about Kate. I'll come as soon as I can.' He opened his wallet and gave her his business card, so she'd have his cell phone number.

Suddenly her eyes glittered with tears, and he saw her throat shift as she swallowed. She nodded. 'Thank you.' Her voice cracked. 'I appreciate that.'

'Sleep well.' He pulled his arm back and the lift doors closed as she walked away.

CHAPTER TEN

'NADIA'S HAD HER BABY, Gran. A little girl.'

Gran's serene expression didn't change.

'She's called her Kate after you. Catherine and Kate. I think it's a gorgeous pairing.'

Isabella had slept for four hours. She'd spoken to her father again, as she had before she'd gone to sleep, and deleted another text from Conlon. Then on the way back to NICU she dropped in to the high dependency ward looking after her grandmother.

'You're a great-grandmother.'

Gran breathed in and out. Her eyes were still shut. Hopefully one day soon they'd open.

'I'm going to see her again now. She weighs two kilograms—that's four pounds four ounces in your terms—and she's gorgeous. Big eyes like Nadia.'

No twitch from Gran and Isabella sighed.

'Still, she's so tiny and fragile-looking. But Simon Purdy—that doctor in the unit I was telling you about—is going to look after her, so I'm happy about that. Turns out he lives one floor up from you.'

The penthouse, she guessed. Funny to think of Simon in a penthouse…

She thought about what she'd said about Simon before to her grandmother.

'And even though I was cross with him yesterday…' Had she been? Yes, actually. She'd been cross that he'd been so cold towards her when she didn't deserve it. She'd still not found out what had upset him. He'd said he'd tell her at breakfast. He hadn't!

'Anyway, he is an excellent paediatrician, and my niece—your great-granddaughter,' she added, trying to break through her grandmother's silence, 'has to have the best. Simon said he would be there whenever Kate needed him.'

She sat back and thought about the relief that gave her. And the fact that Nadia had been pronounced as 'improving' as well. Soon she'd be well enough to visit her baby. It must be so hard for her sister to be stuck in intensive care as a new mum.

'When I phoned just now they said I can see Nadia even though she's still in Intensive Care. I'll have to hurry, because I start work in an hour and a half. I'll drop into the neonatal unit first, and check that Kate's fine, and take a few more photos for Nadia on my phone before I visit her.'

She stood. Looked down at the now familiarly sleeping face.

'It's time you woke up, Gran. We need you to meet your namesake.' She leaned down and kissed the soft wrinkled cheek. 'Love you.'

* * *

When Isabella reached the NICU, she saw Simon, tall and far too eye-catching, beside Carla at Kate's cot. He looked up as she washed her hands at the sink and smiled.

Carla turned Isabella's way as well, as she crossed the room, drying her fingers on a paper towel. 'Congratulations, Auntie,' she said. 'She's beautiful.'

Isabella looked down at the baby with her naso-gastric tube and IV line, and the electronic pulse oximeter sensor strapped to her foot. 'Thank you. She is, isn't she? Has she been a good girl?'

She addressed the last question to Simon, who nodded.

'She's behaving like a typical thirty-two-weeker, so she'll have her moments of unusual interest. But she's stable. Have you seen your sister?'

'I phoned the ward when I woke up. They say she's stable and improving. I thought I'd take a few more photos before I went up. I'm allowed to see her in Intensive Care.'

'She's awake,' Simon said. 'I went up after I'd checked on Kate. I explained Kate's condition and said that we were happy with her.'

Of course he would have done that. Bless him. Not something she would have thought about Simon Purdy a few days ago.

Isabella pressed her lips together to hold back the rush of words. Seemed she was still emotional.

That had been very kind, and she wasn't used to it from him.

'Thank you. She must have been so relieved.'

'She was.' He smiled, and she could see he understood she was still feeling fragile from the fright.

Carla spoke up. 'It's not sensible for you to work this afternoon. You should take the day off today—and tomorrow as well. Family and carer's leave. Though you won't get paid. If you agree, I've found someone to replace you, so no guilt trip needed.'

'Thank you. That would be…' she waved her hand vaguely '…great.' She flicked a glance at Simon and then away—had he asked Carla? 'I'll catch up on sleep.'

'Of course a substitute won't really replace you,' Simon said, and she realised, with a little spurt of shocked amusement, that he was teasing her. Now, that was a first. She furrowed her brows as he grinned and turned back to the cot.

She looked at her boss. 'Thanks, Carla. I was planning on coming in this afternoon, but it's probably safer this way, as I'm still fuzzy from lack of sleep.'

'I do prefer my staff awake,' Carla said mildly. 'No need to rush away after you visit your sister. Take all the time you need and we'll see you as a visiting auntie for the next couple of days.' She tilted her head at Simon. 'As long as Dr Purdy can do without you?

'He managed perfectly well before I came. I'm not worried,' Isabella said dryly. Though it was interesting that Simon had been the first one to suggest she have time off. For someone who had barely spoken to her, he'd made a reversal of interaction with her, even with teasing thrown in. It was all too much to take on board, but right now she didn't want to think about it, because she desperately wanted to see her sister.

Isabella snapped several photos of Kate on her phone—one accidentally, with Simon looking gorgeous in the background. She should delete that, but didn't.

She said her goodbyes, but once she was outside the unit she realised she wasn't sure which way to turn or which floor to get off the lift.

Simon appeared beside her. 'Do you know where you're going?'

'I just realised I don't. I can ask at the reception desk.'

'Follow me. If you don't mind moving fast, I'll show you.' They set off at a rapid pace until they got to the lift. Stepped in. 'I'm going to Theatre to check on a newborn. I'll drop you off on the way.'

'So many words… Who is this chatty person I've met this morning? He's quite a nice fellow.'

'Ha! Nice? I heard he's moody,' Simon said.

Isabella glanced up at him from under her eyebrows. 'Really? Imagine that… I wouldn't have believed it.'

'Cheeky!' Then his voice became more serious. 'What about your parents? Do they know?'

'I rang my father this morning, and then again when I woke up. After I'd spoken to the ICU staff this afternoon. He's flying up tomorrow. Of course he's too busy to come today.'

She heard the underlying bitterness and frowned at herself. It had been unrealistic to expect him to drop everything. She should be used to that now.

'I guess he has to rearrange his schedule,' Simon said, but Isabella could hear the surprise in his voice.

Suddenly she was defensive. 'You should talk. Being married to your job.'

'Not always. I had a life. When I had a wife.'

Suddenly Isabella felt sick. She'd known about that. His loss. His wife. What had she said?

'Heck, Simon, I'm sorry. That was unforgivable of me. But unintended, I promise.'

The doors opened and they stepped out of the lift.

'Don't worry about it. Intensive Care's just there on your left. Say hello to your sister for me.'

He strode on, leaving her feeling like a callous cow.

Damn!

She stared at his rigid back as he disappeared

fast. Then looked back at the closed doors of the intensive care unit. Later she'd find him and apologise.

Again.

CHAPTER ELEVEN

SIMON WINCED AS he sped away from the truth and the pain that slithered around his body like a snake in a box.

Isabella's words had stung. Because it was true. He *had* put his work before his family when Louise was alive. Hell, he'd missed most of the pregnancy, rushing to and from work. She'd never complained. She'd been a saint. And if he'd paid a bit more attention—if he'd been there more—then maybe his wife wouldn't have died alone.

Malachi had told him time and again that nothing could have saved Louise. That it had been quick. An anaphylaxis from a bolus of amniotic fluid, later found in her bloodstream at autopsy, and the allergic response causing rapid cardiac arrest.

But she'd died alone.

And the baby?

Malachi hadn't been so sure, though his friend had said that the chance of survival would have been slim even if someone had been there.

But Simon knew. If he'd been there, his son would have had greater than a fifty-fifty chance. Simon knew that.

If he'd been there, instead of at work, his son might be alive now. They just might have been able to save him from the wreckage of his mother's body before his life was lost.

He knew Isabella hadn't meant to hurt him. But he didn't need anyone else to say it because he reminded himself every morning and every night, getting in and out of bed. The words of his father from long ago—'*It's your fault your mother died giving birth to you.*' And it was his fault for not being there for his wife and child.

Malachi had said he should let it go. And over the last day or so he'd actually thought he was. But it had all crashed back with Isabella's words. Of course he was married his job, and to saving others. He had to make up for the past.

Simon quickened his pace. That was his life. Best thing, really. He needed to work.

Simon left the operating theatre fifteen minutes later. The baby girl he'd gone to see would be transferred to the ward with her mother and he'd check on them both later. After a forceps delivery, the baby had been slow to turn pink after respiration started. But he was confident she had it all worked out now.

He guessed he could go and see Nadia, and ask if she had any questions about Kate, but in his head he knew if she had questions she'd only have to ask her sister.

Still. It couldn't hurt. Any new mother would love to hear about her baby from the baby's doctor. He couldn't avoid Nadia just to avoid seeing Isabella.

Simon felt like slapping his own forehead. He was having so many internal conversations he was twisting himself up in knots.

It all boiled down to the fact that he was being drawn like a lemming to the edge of a cliff—the cliff being Isabella Hargraves—and to the stark reality that he had nothing to offer a woman like her except a sliver of time that would never be enough. And would leave her at risk should she need him.

But Isabella Hargraves had crashed into his world. She would be there in his face at work, in the freaking surf, and even in the lift to his own apartment. The mischievous angels in heaven must be laughing their heads off.

Not his fault. It was fate. He'd tried to stay away.

He pushed open the swing doors to Intensive Care and spoke to one of the nurses there. She told him that Nadia was improving and would probably go to the ward tomorrow morning. He encouraged her to find Nadia a room close to the NICU, and when she agreed to try, he took himself to the sink to wash his hands.

Funny how he couldn't help turning his head towards the room where he knew Nadia had been put… As he'd expected, he noted two blonde heads together.

Isabella was still there. Of course she was. He'd only been gone twenty minutes.

'Here's Simon, now,' he heard her say.

Just hearing that woman speak his name made him stupidly warm.

'Spare me…' he muttered to himself. This was getting out of control. He needed to stop.

He crossed the room and kept his eyes on Isabella's sister. 'How are you feeling, Nadia? Pain under control?'

'I'm getting better all the time.'

Nadia's voice had similarities to Isabella's—he heard them—but her confidence didn't come across as much as Isabella's did.

Could be the fact that Nadia was a patient in a hospital after a traumatic illness and birth.

Or the fact that her husband had died.

He'd discovered she was a widow, and he knew all about that knocking the stuffing out of you. But he suspected it was something else. Perhaps the reason her elder sister was so protective. Had something else happened to Nadia?

He frowned at himself. What was he doing? He should back away from these women and not get more embroiled than he already was.

He didn't want to think about loss. Guilt. Or regret.

'I just dropped in to see if you had any questions. Though I expect your sister can probably answer most of them anyway.'

'None for the moment,' Nadia said, smiling wanly. 'And you're right—Izzy knew the answers to all the ones I had. I loved the photos.'

Izzy? What a travesty to shorten a beautiful name to that. Perhaps Bella? Meaning beautiful. But not Izzy. Sacrilege…

'I sent the pics to her phone,' Isabella said, and he could see in her eyes the anxiety she tried to hide as she watched her sister's tired face. 'As long as you leave it on aeroplane mode, you can look at them as much as you need—until we can get you to her.'

Isabella stood up.

'And on that note…' She kissed her sister's cheek, said softly, 'You need a snooze. I'll be back this afternoon.'

'Say hi to Gran for me,' Nadia whispered, and Isabella nodded.

Mrs Hargraves. Yes. Isabella went every day to see her unconscious grandmother. Somewhere in his chest he felt a twist of empathy that made him want to reach out to her and say he thought she was amazing. She was doing it tough but still thinking of others.

Unlike him. He suspected his attempts at selfish self-preservation hadn't helped her at all this last week. It was hard to remember that she'd only begun in the unit such a short time ago. It felt as if he'd been watching her for way longer.

Simon saw a man in the dark suit striding

swiftly towards them and his mouth quirked up. One of the ICU nurses followed the newcomer, trying to catch him up with a chart.

'Malachi.' Simon held out his hand and his friend shook it warmly.

'Simon. Come to see my patient, have you?' Malachi leaned past Simon and smiled at Nadia in the bed. 'I won't stay long and interrupt your visitors,' he told her.

CHAPTER TWELVE

MALACHI MADDEN, THE man Isabella had seen when Nadia had first been admitted, was clearly Simon's friend. He looked nice, if in a hurry, and she recognised the consultant's fierce intelligence and wanted all those brains directed at her sister.

'Nice to meet you, again.' she murmured. 'Thank you for looking after my sister so well. Please don't rush—I'm just leaving.'

Before she could move past him, Simon said to Malachi, 'Isabella is one of the NICU nurses in our unit here. And a midwife.'

'Yes, I know. Nice to meet you again, Isabella.' He glanced at Simon and raised his brows, with a twinkle in his intelligent eyes. 'I've heard the team are pretty good down there.' She watched their rapport. It was easy and were obviously used to teasing each other.

Isabella glanced at Simon. 'Yes. We're very fortunate.'

Simon said, 'Do you remember Mrs Hargraves? That friend of your grandmother's who lives in the flat below me?'

Malachi frowned, and then nodded. 'She was injured in that nasty hit-and-run accident a month or so ago. Millicent was very distressed to hear about it.'

'Nadia and Isabella are her granddaughters.'

Malachi's face softened, as did his voice. 'Oh… How is she? I heard she's still unconscious?'

Isabella didn't know what to say. Why had Simon shared this? She scrambled for a short response. 'Yes, she hasn't woken up yet. I see her every day.'

'Of course.' Malachi nodded. His face was serious. 'I would visit if it were me, too. I must tell my grandmother. You should come and meet my wife, Lisandra,' he told her, with a searching look towards his friend and then a smile. 'Simon, you should come too. Isabella, maybe you can convince him to arrive for dinner instead of dessert.'

What? Dinner? With Simon? She felt as if she'd just been steamrollered.

Malachi raised his eyebrows at his friend. 'If you're done with Nadia, trot away with Isabella so I can see my patient.'

Isabella closed her mouth on the open sag it wanted to make. 'Goodbye, Dr Madden.'

He nodded vaguely, as if he'd already forgotten her, and walked instantly over to Nadia and took her wrist.

She didn't realise Simon was behind her until she went to open the swing doors out of the ICU and he stretched out his arm ahead of her and pushed the door until she was through.

'He's funny,' she said.

'Malachi is no-nonsense and a very good friend. We went through med school together.'

She still didn't understand Simon's blurting out of information. 'Why did you tell him about Gran?'

'No idea... I'm sorry if I shouldn't have. I think maybe because I think you'd like Lisandra, and I think you need a friend right now. She's also a midwife. You have that in common. They have twin boys who just turned one.'

'Good grief. How does she manage when he works all hours as an obstetrician?'

'Lisandra is one of the calmest women I know. As well as the best thing that's ever happened to Malachi—for which I am very grateful.'

She still didn't understand why he'd shared so much about her and Nadia with his friend. 'What made you think of my grandmother when you were talking to him?'

'I remember meeting Mrs Hargraves and Malachi's grandmother, Millicent, in the lift one day. Now, Millicent...she's a terrifying lady.'

Isabella couldn't imagine Simon being terrified by any woman. But she suspected he meant the comment fondly. His eyes twinkled.

Something made her ask, 'Do *you* have a terrifying grandmother?'

'I don't have any grandmother. Or a mother.'

There was darkness there in those words. Sorrow. Regret. Something she wanted to find out more about.

'In fact,' Simon went on, 'Malachi's the closest thing I have to a relative and he's not even blood-related.'

Oh… More sadness. Simon had baggage she hadn't even considered.

'I'm sorry to hear that. My family might not win any happy-all-together awards, but at least I have them.'

'Yes—and they have you.' He cast a sideways glance at her as they walked to the lift. 'I'm beginning to see that you're the person who worries about everyone else.'

How the heck had he deduced that? It wasn't true. Was it? He barely knew her. And apart from Nadia, he didn't know her family at all.

The lift arrived and deposited them on the ground floor. 'Are you coming to check on Kate before you go home?' he asked.

And suddenly she was awkward again. 'I'd like to. Is that okay? Even though I'm not working?'

He waved her in. 'Of course. You're officially a relative. Next of kin to his mother. You can visit any time.'

It still didn't feel right to go outside of regular visiting times. 'But there are specific visiting hours for non-staff members. I don't want to be a nuisance.'

He wrinkled his brow at her, as if he couldn't

believe what she was saying. 'I don't think there's any risk of you abusing your position.'

And he held the door open for her so she had no choice. Not that she wanted one.

Shoulder to shoulder, they washed their hands at the sink until Simon, who'd finished first, tore off some paper towel and then went off to see Carla.

Isabella crossed the busy unit, past open cots and rolling cots, and past the staff working on the tiny inhabitants of both, to check on Kate.

Her niece lay on her belly, leads sneaking from under her chest at each side. Her left foot now sported the pulse oximeter probe that had previously been attached to the right foot. She was sleeping and serene. Warm under her heater. Her breathing steady and sure.

Isabella's quick survey of the monitors suggested her vital signs were stable. She picked up the chart, not sure whether she was allowed to, but not letting that stop her.

She confirmed everything looked normal for the moment, though she suspected a tinge of yellowing jaundice in Kate's skin. She expected there'd be a need for phototherapy soon, to assist her body to rid itself of the extra bilirubin. And the use of purple lights to help disperse the toxic by-products.

Once born into the outside air, babies normally discarded unneeded extra oxygen-carrying blood cells. But, as Kate was a prem, her liver would struggle to break down the products left behind. Hence the build up of jaundice.

Simon didn't need her mentioning it—he'd already be on top of it all—and it was truly strange how relaxed she was feeling about Kate's progress. There were still so many obstacles that could catch her tiny niece out as she grew, like infections and breathing difficulties, or a need for nasogastric feeds of expressed breast milk—something she and Nadia had discussed and would address again this afternoon.

It was almost a shock, how calm she felt now that Simon was in charge of Kate's care. How reassured. Though his very competent registrar would have been just as good. She needed to remember that.

It just went to show that sometimes too much knowledge could be a problem.

Maybe she should go home before she said something else out of line. Again.

She would drop in to Gran as well—tell her about Malachi Madden's grandmother. Maybe that would be something that might stimulate her.

Then she'd have a sleep herself, she supposed, and she'd better polish Gran's flat and clean the bathroom in case her father decided to stay there. But knowing him, he'd book a suite at the nearest hotel, so he could be on his own. That was more his style. But maybe she'd have a chance to be his host and they could really talk.

Who knew when he would come? He hadn't known himself when she'd last spoken to him. But she couldn't help being glad that he would. For Nadia. For Gran. And for her. Because if it wasn't for Simon she would be feeling very alone amongst all these medical dramas.

Simon…the kind-eyed Simon…who was suddenly her friend.

Simon returned with Carla and Isabella felt awkward again. In the way. Superfluous. Without a real job. A third wheel because she wasn't working this afternoon.

'I'm going now,' she told them.

Simon frowned, as if he'd read her thoughts, and she saw him close his mouth as if he was about to say something.

Carla lifted her head from a chart. 'I'm sure we'll see you later.'

Isabella nodded. She glanced once more at her niece and then left, feeling suddenly rootless.

CHAPTER THIRTEEN

SIMON'S GAZE FOLLOWED Isabella as she opened the door and left. There was something about the droop in her shoulders that hinted she felt a little lost.

Funny how much that thought troubled him.

Which was a very good reason for him to turn around and concentrate on the baby in front of him.

'Do I sense a change with you and Isabella?' Carla's voice was quietly discreet, and didn't carry, yet he wished she hadn't voiced the question at all. It meant that others could see that things were noteworthy between them.

'No. Not really.' He lowered his brows at her, but she knew him too well to be bothered. 'Why would you ask that?'

'Uh...because everybody can feel the friction between you two and it would be good if you could clear the air.'

He huffed. 'I have. We had breakfast together this morning and I apologised for my moodiness with her.'

'Simon, I'm impressed.' But her eyes twinkled and he suspected she was more amused than impressed. 'That was brave.'

He pulled a face. 'That's the end of this topic.

Back to work,' he mock-growled, and Carla dipped her head to hide her smile.

Simon pointed to the prem in front of them. 'I think Kate's becoming jaundiced. I'll order a serum bilirubin. Has she started on EBM yet?'

'Yes. Mum's started expressing and the ICU sent down the first colostrum. You happy for us to start that?'

'Absolutely. ASAP. The usual regime.'

Carla made a note. 'Yes, we'll gradually increase the expressed milk and decrease the IV if she tolerates it.'

'Has she passed meconium?'

'Yes. And voided twice. Clever baby.'

All looking good for the moment, then. The extra relief he felt was interesting.

'Excellent. All systems working. Let me know if there's problems. Tell the night staff to ring through straight to me for Kate.' He avoided meeting Carla's raised brows. 'Anyone else you're worried about?' he asked.

'Nope. All up to date. We'll let you know if we need you.'

'Fine. I'll head to my rooms, then. I've got appointments all afternoon, so I'll be there if you need me.'

By four-thirty Simon was with his last patient.

Young Reece had unstable diabetes. He was

thrilled with his new insulin pump, which meant he could play with the other kids more than he'd ever been able to before.

Simon had known Reece for the last three years, and always enjoyed talking to the boy and his mother.

By five p.m. he was waving them farewell at the door, and he was just about to head for the children's ward when his phone rang.

'Dr Purdy.' Malachi was in good spirits, it seemed.

'Dr Madden. You sound chipper.'

'My wife requests the pleasure of your company tomorrow night for dinner.'

'Does she? Are you home from work already, Malachi? Things have certainly changed.'

Malachi had been worse than Simon for staying at work all hours.

'You should try it,' his friend said. 'The twins are waving at you. They want to see their uncle Simon.'

Simon shook his head. But he couldn't stop the big smile on his face. 'Who are you? What happened to the workaholic?'

But Simon knew what had happened. Lisandra had changed his friend's life, and his priorities, for the better. And even though the twins weren't Malachi's, he adored his new family and revelled in being a father.

Malachi said, 'I've seen the light. So, how

about you shift your last appointment and get your rounds done early tomorrow?'

Simon considered that. 'My secretary hasn't left, yet. I'll see what I can do.'

'Lisandra said to bring Isabella.'

Good grief. Malachi—or Lisandra, more likely—was matchmaking, and the idea scared the daylights out of him.

'I'm not sure about Isabella's shifts.' Except he knew she was off. He'd seen the staff rota.

'How about you give me her number and Lisandra can ring her? Midwives stick together, you know.'

Malachi wasn't fazed or worried about Simon's feelings. It wasn't in his make-up—and hadn't Simon accepted that years ago?

Served him right. He'd been the one to tell Isabella she would like Malachi's wife. But now it was happening, old doubts and insecurities slithered in. Was this really a good idea? The one situation he'd thought he wouldn't bump into Isabella was socially, with Malachi. Now Malachi was changing that.

Without permission, the words slipped out. 'Seems there won't be anywhere I can go and not meet this woman.'

'Explain?'

Simon sighed. Bowing to the inevitable. 'She lives in her grandmother's flat—which, as you know, is one floor below mine. We work together in the NICU. And guess what she does in her off time.'

Malachi laughed. 'Don't tell me…she's a surfer.'

'Yep.'

Malachi laughed again. 'I can't wait to tell Lisandra.'

Simon couldn't help smiling. Not so long ago even one Malachi laugh would have been a reason for celebration.

'Tell me what…?' Simon heard Lisandra ask in the background.

'Simon's being stalked by a midwife.'

Simon grimaced as Lisandra laughed. 'I am not. She didn't even know any of those things.'

Malachi chuckled. 'Who knew Simon's relationships could be so much fun? Six p.m. You'll be kicked out at eight. You know we like to go to bed early.'

The phone went dead.

Simon stared at the receiver in his hand and gritted his teeth. Served him right for dumping all that information about Isabella on his friend. Malachi wasn't stupid—too freakin' smart. But usually not so intuitive.

Of course introducing and giving the back story on a woman was out of character for Simon.

Too late. Lisandra had the run of it now.

He shrugged and went to make peace with his

secretary about changing his appointment times tomorrow, then took himself off to the children's ward.

After work that night, Simon took his car from the garage underneath the building and did something he hadn't done for a long time. He went to the cemetery where they'd buried Louise and Lucas, his son who had never breathed.

It was sunset. And between the trees lay shadows. Although above the canopy the sky was alight with an orange glow that made the headstones sparkle as the last rays sank into the sandstone blocks.

He walked to the row he needed, and six graves along, until he came to Louise and Lucas's. There. A cold stone where once a sweet woman and the promise of a young life had been.

Just twenty-eight, and so gentle in spirit had been his kind and loving wife. He'd thought that there would never be another woman for him. That what they'd had was too special. Too perfect.

But mostly it had involved too much guilt.

Because the ending had been anything but perfect.

She'd been so happy in her pregnancy. And he couldn't remember how many times since her death he'd railed at himself for not spending more time at home with her.

Three years. A long time to mourn. Or not long enough?

His friends had been pushing him to look for happiness again, but he'd felt so guilty. So disloyal. So uninterested.

Until now. When suddenly he was swamped by the feelings that were growing for Isabella Hargraves. What if he let them flower? What was his plan? To fall in love again? Have a baby again? Already his head was shaking at the thought. What if he lost another wife? What if Isabella died in childbirth?

No. He couldn't. He wasn't ready.

CHAPTER FOURTEEN

ISABELLA'S PHONE BUZZED with a text at six o'clock that evening.

Hello, Isabella. My name is Lisandra Madden. Is this a good time to call you?

Isabella read it again. Then she remembered Malachi Madden inviting her and Simon for dinner.

Good grief. They didn't let any grass grow underfoot.

She texted back.

Now is fine.

The phone rang within ten seconds.

'Thanks for the quick response,' came a lilting woman's voice. 'It's Lisandra here. I've got twin boys and they're asleep at the moment. I try to do everything in the quiet times.'

I bet you do.

Isabella could imagine. And she smiled at the thought.

'Malachi tells me you're a midwife and new to the area. He also says you work with Simon Purdy. Well, those boys are great friends, and it's always a struggle to get Simon to come out. We're having a dinner party tomorrow night. Malachi's grandmother will be there, and we'd like to invite you both as well—if you're up to it.'

Before Isabella could answer Lisandra said quickly, 'It won't be a late night. We call them "six to eight" parties.'

Isabella laughed—how funny—and replied, 'I'd probably run on the same hours if I had twins.'

She could absolutely fit that in.

'My father is flying up tomorrow, to see my sister, but he won't be here till late. I've been invited to his hotel at nine, and I was wondering what I'd do until then.'

'Good grief, we'll all be snoring by that time,' Lisandra murmured with disbelief.

Isabella laughed again. She liked this woman already. 'Then thank you. What can I bring tomorrow?'

'If you can bring Simon on time, I'd be very grateful. The man doesn't seem to know the meaning of punctuality. Everything else is covered. I'll text you the address, in case Simon gets called away. You can park underneath the apartments in the visitors' parking and then take the lift straight up—I'll send you the codes.'

'You've thought of everything.'

'Good. I'm looking forward to meeting you. I haven't had a good chat with a midwife for ages.'

'I'm more of a neonatal nurse, right now. But I look forward to meeting you too.'

'Great. Bye.'

'Bye.'

Good grief, Isabella thought as the call ended. A whirlwind had just blown past, and she'd been caught up in it. She wondered what Simon thought about going with her to dinner. Her mouth twitched.

Someone knocked on her door.

Was she about to find out?

There weren't many in the block who knew her well enough to knock on her door.

Isabella peered through the peephole and saw Simon on the other side, staring off to the left.

Yep. She was about to find out Simon's response to the dinner invitation.

While she watched, he lifted his hand to the back of his neck and rubbed. *Tired or uncomfortable?* she wondered, and opened the door.

'Hello.' She opened her mouth to say more, when a horrible thought crashed into her. 'Nadia…? Kate…?'

'Both fine,' Simon said quickly. 'If they weren't I would have phoned immediately.'

She blew her breath out. 'Of course. Sorry—mild panic attack came up out of nowhere.'

'I get it. But I'm here about Malachi and Lisandra…' He put his hand over his face as if he was embarrassed. 'Have you had the call yet?'

She opened the door wider and swept out her arm to indicate that he could come in. 'Yes, I've just finished. Lisandra's a force to be reckoned with.'

'Lisandra's a delight, but when she's determined on something, it's hard to get away.'

She chewed her lip to stop the smile. 'My task is to get you there on time,' she said.

'Well, I'm to take you and a bottle of wine.' He met her gaze fully, concern in his. 'So, you're okay with this?'

'Sure. Sounds like fun.' She smiled reassuringly at him. He looked as if he needed it. 'My father is arriving tomorrow night, and I'm to meet him at nine at his hotel. Saves me sitting here, watching the clock.'

She saw his gaze slide over the room. And the hallway beyond. 'He's not going to stay here with you? It's three bedrooms, isn't it?'

She sighed. 'Yes. And I've just cleaned in case he comes.' She shrugged. 'But no. He'll feel much more comfortable arriving late at a hotel.' She could see that he thought she might be hurt by her father's choice. 'It's fine with me. I told you we don't do *happy-all-together*.'

He nodded and she went on.

'I'm a little bit nervous about meeting Malachi's terrifying grandmother now you've told me about her.'

Simon laughed. 'Oh, she'll love you. You won't have any problems.'

And what did she do now? With Simon in her flat? Looking scrumptious. With the scent of freshly showered man, damp hair and that subtle woodsy cologne she was coming to recognise.

'Would you like a drink? Tea? Coffee?'

'Tea would be great. Black. No sugar, thanks.'

Same as her. And why would that make her want to happy dance? Weird…

She flicked the kettle on. 'Got it.' She started rifling through the cupboards. 'I think I've got some biscuits here.'

'No, it's fine. My housekeeper leaves me dinner in the fridge to heat up.'

That made her pause, her hand on the cupboard door. 'You have a housekeeper?'

'I spend a fair bit of time at work.'

He looked just a little embarrassed, and that made her smile. As if he was a bad person for not wanting to keep house.

'I'd rather surf waves than clean.'

She nodded. She thought of her afternoon of rubber gloves and bathrooms and grimaced. 'Me too. Speaking of surfing… Have you had a chance to get back out there since yesterday morning?'

'Was that only yesterday morning?' His hand pinched the bridge of his nose. 'It feels like a year ago.'

She narrowed her eyes at him. 'I've been thinking about that.' She poured boiling water into a cup. 'And I have a theory.'

'Oh, yeah?' He took the cup from her, removed the teabag and put it in the bin.

She liked the fact that he was making himself at home here, opening cupboards until he found the garbage.

'Yes, I think the reason you were bad-tempered with me at work is because I was surfing in your spot.'

'I don't own the surf.'

But it sounded as if he wished he did.

Then he smiled. Held out his hands in a *What can I do?* gesture. 'I told myself you were an incredibly intelligent woman and I'd have to stay at the top of my game.'

'True.' She nodded slowly. 'You do. Is the rest true, you were bad tempered because I was surfing in your spot?'

'I confess.'

'The ocean is big enough for both of us,' she mused.

He was watching her. 'It should be.' There was a small, ironic smile on his mouth. 'But if I want to try not to expose myself to the fact that I find my new colleague compellingly and breath-stealingly attractive, it's very difficult when she pops up not only at work, but also in the one place I go to escape work.'

She opened her mouth, but he held up his hand.

'Oh, it gets worse. She even lives in the same block as I do.'

She opened her mouth again.

He said, 'And one more thing. Let's add to that. My friends have now included her in their circle. So, I'm going to be exposed to Isabella Hargraves in every part of my day.'

'Poor you,' she said.

'Or poor you? I'm not cross any more, because I've given up fighting the inevitable.

That made her blink. 'What's the inevitable?.'

Did she sound petulant?

'Being drawn to you. Attracted. You know you're delightful.'

He must have seen her brows draw up into her hairline. Because he went on.

'And, yes, I would like to be your friend. Please.' The humour left his face. 'I need to say that because of the past I'm in no hurry to be more than that. And I think it's only fair that I tell you I live for my work.'

Wow. That was pretty brave. And a downer. Because she was attracted right back, and he was married to his work. Still, she appreciated his honesty—even if she was a little bit disappointed.

But she had the feeling this was a big admission for Simon. So she held out her hand. 'To friendship.'

CHAPTER FIFTEEN

SIMON TOOK ISABELLA'S slender hand in his and solemnly held it. Her fingers felt warm, silky, and suddenly fragile in his. He didn't want to let go. But he had to. Now. He'd ease his fingers away as soon as they weren't Velcroed onto hers.

'Are you surfing tomorrow?' he asked.

She pulled her hand away, picked up her mug and sat at the small table.

'Yes, because I don't have to go to work. Thanks to Dr Simon Purdy, who has told my supervisor that I require two days FACS leave.'

He laughed. 'I did do that.'

'Well, I appreciate it. Thank you. I would have pushed myself to turn up, but it wouldn't have been a sensible thing to do with no sleep.'

'They're moving Nadia down to a room near the NICU tomorrow. Did you know that?'

Her face lit up and he saw again her love for her sister.

'No. That's good. She's still improving, then?'

'Blood pressure is settling well.'

'And my niece?'

'I'd say she'll be under phototherapy by tonight.'

'I thought that.' She nodded and he could see she'd expected it.

'You didn't say anything.'

Her mouth kinked up and drew his gaze.

That mouth.

'I have great faith in you. But I would have said something tomorrow,' she told him.

He laughed and thought, *Oh, yeah, I'll have to watch myself, or I could fall hard for this woman.*

He was not going to do that—for her sake, not his.

At five forty-five the next evening, after he'd ensured Isabella's sister and niece were both stable and improving, and he'd dressed appropriately enough to satisfy Malachi's grandmother, Simon pressed the bell on Isabella's door.

The NICU had been busy today, with the new admission of twins at thirty-four weeks. But he'd put Henry in charge and suggested, for once, that he only be called for his own patients instead of the usual—being called by anyone who needed him for a paediatric consult.

The door opened and Isabella stood there, stealing his breath, then his words. And he hoped not his heart, as his chest felt clamped in a vice that made cardiac output difficult.

'You look beautiful…' The words escaped in an awed murmur.

And, my glory, she did. The flowing silk trousers and jacket floated over a cream blouse in soft shades of lilac that brought out the green of her eyes while they hugged and skimmed the length of her body. The feather-light material shifted alluringly as she moved.

Her gaze skimmed his outfit and then finished at his face. 'Looking good yourself, Dr Purdy. I like the Tigger tie. And you're right on time.'

She pulled the door shut behind her. He stifled disappointment. So, he wasn't going in?

'Malachi's boys like this tie,' he said, struggling for normal conversation. A 'date' with Isabella was having way more impact than he'd been prepared for.

They'd finally agreed the previous evening to go in her car, against Simon's preference. She'd argued that she was driving on to the hotel afterwards to see her father. She would drop him home on her way.

Now, as he waited beside the driver's door for her to unlock the car, she slanted a sideways look at him. 'Are you planning on driving my car?'

The lock clicked and he reached down. 'No, I'm opening your door for you.'

She lifted her head and laughed up at him. The sound was sexy as hell, and sent blood pounding all over his body in ways he'd forgotten existed.

'Well, thank you, kind sir.' She pulled her beautiful mouth into order, as if holding back more mirth. 'Do I have to come round to your side and open *your* door?'

'It would have been easier if we'd taken my car,' he said.

'But not more sensible.'

'And if I get called out?'

She shrugged, with a *not my problem* attitude he also found sexy.

He sighed. 'It's close… I can always get a taxi.'

She settled into her seat. 'Or I can drive you. Let's go.'

He closed her door, his mouth twitching, because he was so unused to this kind of rapport where she could fire back. Shaking his head at his own smitten-ness, he walked around the car. It was cleaned and polished enough to show she cared about it.

'Nice car,' he said as he climbed in.

'This is Rosa.' Isabella patted the leather dashboard. 'She's my friend. Buckle up.'

Once Simon had himself settled, trying not to deep-breathe the now familiar scent of her delicate perfume, Isabella pulled smoothly out of the garage and into the busy street.

It was still light outside, and there were families wandering across the road to the beach and people dog-walking after work. Her driving style was smooth and confident, like everything about her, and he could feel himself relax. Maybe he could cope with her driving. Louise had been a timid nightmare…

She glanced at him. 'So how did Malachi and Lisandra meet? Was she working as a midwife?'

Simon laughed. He couldn't help it. It was funny. Though he was sure it hadn't been at the time.

Isabella turned her beautiful face his way briefly and arched her brows. 'Was it that good a meet-cute?'

Meet-cute? He'd seen that movie. Ha!

'They met in a stuck elevator at the hospital. Lisandra's waters had broken and Malachi almost delivered the twins in there.'

Thankfully they'd pulled up at a red light. Because he could see his driver was having trouble concentrating.

Something lodged in his chest as she stared at him. She looked so cute, blinking incredulous green eyes at him. Then she turned back to the road. He could see the smile on her face, and he just had to lean forward to see her full expression, not just in profile.

He felt as if he could actually see her imagining the scenario. 'Crazy, huh?'

She inhaled with amusement. 'That's different…'

'There's a long story there that's not mine to tell, but they're the happiest couple I know. Lisandra changed Malachi's life for the better, and for that I'll always be grateful to her.'

'Well, I'm sure he's changed hers too. He seems very nice.'

'He is.'

They drove through busy Coolangatta, along the beachfront and around the headland to Kira Beach. The waves rolled in as the road curved around the bay.

He pointed. 'The underground car park is up ahead. Just past the lights. Yep, turn left here.'

They pulled under a tall white building with beautiful gardens full of red hibiscus in flower.

He watched her press the code numbers into the keypad and the boom gate lifted smoothly, so they could drive past and park beside the elevators in the visitors' parking.

'If I ever come back here to visit Lisandra, I'll know how to find the place.'

He hoped she would. 'It's easier for her to have visitors here, with the boys, than it is for them to go out.'

They went to the lifts, and he pressed in the code, and then she was next to him again in another closed space. Alone. Just the two of them. Close.

There would be time for a kiss, his crazy inner demon told him, as he stared straight ahead at the doors.

Diversion needed. His mouth dried and he had to moisten it before he could speak.

'You'll enjoy the view from Malachi's apartment.'

When the lift doors opened, they were in an entry foyer with only one closed front door. Thankfully, as he stepped out, Simon could breathe again. He took a couple of extra, subtle inhalations before he knocked.

CHAPTER SIXTEEN

A BLONDE WOMAN in her late twenties opened the door, leaned forward and kissed Simon's cheek. This had to be Lisandra, Isabella thought. She had a fine bone structure, a pink bow of a mouth and big, deep turquoise eyes.

'Simon. Welcome.' She smiled at Isabella, her face warm and happy. 'And you must be Isabella.' The woman kissed her cheek too. 'That's for getting him here on time.' She laughed at Simon and ushered them in, saying, 'It's so lovely to meet you. I'm Lisandra. Come in… Come in… Malachi is just bathing the boys.'

And after that whirlwind introduction, reminiscent of the phone call she'd shared with Malachi's wife, Isabella just knew she could become firm friends with this woman.

Their hosts' apartment seemed to stretch for ever—probably because the sea air flowed seamlessly through open sliding doors to a wide terrace instead of a narrow balcony. She guessed there was a big drop to the ground below, but in front of them the horizon stretched over the waves.

White marble tiles ran from the floor to the terrace rail, past white furniture with blue accents, a wall-length television screen and a small curved bar with stools.

'Come through and meet Malachi's grandmother, Millicent. She's out on the terrace.'

A tall woman, possibly in her early eighties, stepped away from the rail and turned their way. Not quite as tall as Malachi, she was wearing peach silk trousers and a paler peach sleeveless tunic, almost white. The silk draped softly over her reed-thin body. Her make-up glowed with perfection, and her short, curly, snow-white hair was artfully tousled. Her smile shone warm and genuine as she came towards them.

'Simon,' she said, and her voice was huskier than Isabella had expected. 'A pleasure as always to see you.'

She kissed his cheeks in the French style, but her eyes were on Isabella.

'My dear, you have a look of your grandmother—those fine eyes and cheekbones. I'm Millicent Charles. A friend of Catherine's.'

It felt so long since she'd heard someone actually refer to her grandmother by her first name and a lump formed in her throat. She swallowed and smiled. 'It's lovely to meet you, Mrs Charles.'

'Likewise. And, please, call me Millicent. I've been so distressed since Catherine's accident. Any sign of improvement? I've asked your father, but he had nothing to offer.'

Isabella tried not to wince. *Yes, that sounded like dear old Dad*, Isabella thought grimly.

'She's breathing for herself. The hospital is

maintaining intravenous nutrition. And…' she spread her hands '…we're just waiting.'

'Malachi says you visit often?'

Had they been talking about her? No, probably just about Gran. And it was good to talk about her grandmother with someone who knew her.

'I visit every day. Sometimes I think she can hear me. Hopefully I'm not driving her mad with my chatter.'

Kind, yet faded eyes shared sympathy and understanding. 'I'm very sure she loves your visits.'

'Well, I told her yesterday that I would be meeting you tonight. Now I can tell her tomorrow that I did.'

'Excellent. Would you mind if I visited her as well? I didn't get the impression from your father that it would be possible.'

'He's arriving tonight. I'll make sure he knows that your visits certainly are permitted. The staff have been wonderful at welcoming me. She has an IV, and monitors, of course, but nothing that jumps out at you too much. I think it's a lovely idea.'

Malachi appeared out of a side hallway, carrying two blonde-headed toddlers in zip-up sleep suits, one in each arm. One of the boys leaned towards Simon as they drew close, and Simon scooped him out of his father's hold and perched him against his chest.

Malachi leaned across and shook Simon's hand. He smiled at Isabella. 'Welcome to our home.'

Lisandra lifted the other little boy from his father and perched him on her hip. 'Isabella, these are our boys, Bastian and Bennett. Bennett is the one who grabbed his uncle Simon.'

The little boy had caught Simon's tie and was tugging it.

'That's his favourite tie. Simon bought him a stuffed Tigger and Bastian a stuffed Winnie-the-Pooh bear, which they sleep with.'

And there was Simon—gorgeous Dr Simon Purdy—so at ease and delighted with the little boy in his arms. Of course, he was a paediatrician, so he was good with kids. But, dammit, she could see him being a fabulous dad with a pack of his own.

Except he'd said he would never marry again or be a dad. That was sad. For him. Not for her. That tragic fact had nothing to do with her. But her heart still hurt.

Millicent had taken herself to one of the large white sofas, and Lisandra carried Bastian across to her and settled him in her lap. His grandmother tucked her chin down to talk to the boy, and for a minute Isabella thought she was going to cry.

That was what she wanted Gran to do. She wanted Gran to be there for Nadia's baby, like she'd been there for Isabella and Nadia. Like Malachi's grandmother.

Why couldn't her grandmother be here, too? She'd already lost her mother. She wasn't ready to lose Gran.

Isabella felt a sympathetic touch on her shoulder. A touch that filled her with comfort and strength. Then Simon lifted his hand and let it fall. He had followed her gaze. As if he knew what she was thinking. She shoved the emotion away. He couldn't have. But she glanced at him with gratitude because that touch had helped.

'Come through to the kitchen, Isabella.' Lisandra intruded on her thoughts as well, and she was glad to step away from the sadness. Maybe not so glad to step away from Simon's side…

'I'd love to. What can I do to help?'

And that was how the evening went. Every time she felt even a tiny bit sad, or a little out of place amongst these people who knew each other so very well, Lisandra was there to bring her into the conversation or ask her a question. Or Simon would catch her eye and smile. Touch her briefly. Make sure she didn't feel as if he didn't understand.

When the meal was over, Isabella helped Lisandra stack the dishwasher while Malachi and Simon took the boys to their bedroom to read them a story.

'There's no excuse for you not to visit me,' said Lisandra. 'You know where I live and now you know all the codes.'

'And I have your phone number,' Isabella agreed, with a grin.

'While the boys are little, I'm not thinking about going back to work.' She dropped the volume of her voice so she wouldn't be overheard. 'Malachi would be happy if I never went back to work, but I loved being a midwife.'

'It is special,' Isabella agreed.

Lisandra shrugged. 'No rush. I'll get there. Malachi says you work in the neonatal nursery?'

'Yes, with Simon. He's very good. The unit's excellent.'

Lisandra's bright eyes closed briefly. 'It is. And I know. We had a scare with Bastian and Simon was there for us.'

'I'm sorry to hear that.'

Lisandra glanced towards the bedrooms. 'We try not to think about it.'

'Then don't.' Isabella changed the subject. 'Simon's looking after my sister's prem baby.'

'That's right. You're an auntie. First time?'

'Yes. And a first grandchild for my dad.'

She hadn't really thought about that, and wondered if there was any chance Kate could change him into a more human, human being.

'You said your father's arriving tonight?'

'Nine o'clock,' Isabella confirmed.

'I won't even be awake to think of you.' Lisandra mimed sleep.

'Yes, but you're a lot busier than I am.'

Lisandra shrugged. 'I'm not working… Malachi tells me you surf?'

'Yes, I've just found out Simon does too.'

There was a definite sparkle in Lisandra's eyes. 'I know… Are you good at it?'

Isabella knew she was good. But she didn't boast. 'Good enough to enjoy it.'

'Will you teach me?'

Ah… Hence the questions? 'Of course. I'd love to. My grandmother taught me.'

Lisandra looked ridiculously happy. 'That's a date, then.'

Malachi and Simon returned to sit with Millicent in the lounge room, and the women joined them there. Lisandra touched her husband's arm, her fingers resting lightly on his shirtsleeve, and they shared a smile. The look of connection in their faces made Isabella look away. She wanted that too. Connection. Silent communication.

Her thoughts stilled. Narrowed. Wasn't that what Simon had been giving her all night?

Dimly she heard Lisandra say, 'Are the boys asleep?'

'Out for the count.' There was a satisfied smile in Malachi's voice.

'Then I'm going to show Isabella the angels through the doorway.'

Lisandra took her arm, and they turned left up the corridor to where a door stood ajar at the end.

Soft light spilled into the hallway. It had an odd bluish tinge.

Isabella leaned her head around the doorway and could see a blue nightlight shaped like a fish-bowl, with tiny imitation fish swimming in a blue ball. The light allowed her to see two blond heads on the pillows in twin beds. One tiny boy was tucked under his cover with his Tigger, and the other had already thrown his quilt off, one arm flung out, holding his Winnie the Pooh.

Isabella stepped back. Mouthed, *They are gorgeous.*

Lisandra smiled and drew her back down the corridor. She sighed theatrically. 'Even more so when they're asleep.'

It wasn't much later when Simon stood up. 'Gone eight o'clock. Looks like it's time for us to be kicked out.'

Malachi glanced at his watch. 'Oh, you sneaked in an extra five minutes there. Luckily someone was watching.'

Simon laughed. 'Did you bring your car, Millicent, or would you like a lift?'

Isabella lifted her head to smile.

Simon put his fingers over his face and dragged them down comically. 'I mean would you like a lift in Isabella's car, because she won the discussion on who was driving tonight.'

Millicent smiled approvingly at Isabella. 'I have

my own vehicle, thank you.' She nodded. 'Always good to keep them guessing who's boss.'

'It's a democracy,' Simon said dryly, and shook Malachi's hand.

Millicent laughed.

'Dinner was wonderful, as always.'

Simon kissed Lisandra's cheek and stood waiting patiently for Isabella to say her goodbyes.

It had been perfect, Isabella thought. Not a boring dinner party at all like her father's events.

Everything had been a pleasure, and she thought Lisandra might be one of the luckiest people she knew.

'Thank you so much for a wonderful evening.'

'First of many, hopefully,' Malachi said briskly.

Lisandra hugged her. 'Ring me when you're ready for a surf on a weekend. Malachi and Simon can mind the boys.'

Suddenly she and Simon were standing close together again, in the lift going down to the car park. She felt as if she'd glimpsed a family the like of which she wanted so badly her heart and arms ached with emptiness. But it did feel like that warmth would never be hers.

'Did you enjoy that?' Simon asked, and Isabella turned her eyes to him.

She couldn't articulate how much. Instead, she nodded and asked, 'Did you?'

His tie looked crumpled, where Bennett had mashed it with his pudgy fingers and Simon had tried to straighten it. It needed an iron. She leaned across and tugged it, to pull the creases out, and then stepped back. That had brought her very close to him. She probably shouldn't have done it.

He was looking at her quizzically, and she hurried into speech. 'It was a wonderful night. I love your friends—and Millicent is wonderful.'

Two 'wonderfuls'? Brain, brain...where is my brain?

She concentrated on the evening, because that was safer than dwelling on the fact that the lift was slow, and that they were alone in the small space. And that she'd just touched him without invitation.

His shoulders loomed next to her but it wasn't just his big body taking up space—it was his personality. The one she'd seen tonight. The friend. The uncle. The charming escort. The man who cared if she felt sad. She almost couldn't believe that side of him.

Thankfully the lift had arrived at the underground car park, so she stepped out, unlocked her car, slid past Simon's door-opening arm, and sat behind the wheel as her mind mulled over the conundrum of her thoughts.

Earlier, she hadn't noticed being overwhelmed by Simon in the car because she'd been driving. But watching Simon tonight, listening to his jokes with Malachi, seeing his kindnesses and the way he'd handled the little boys, as if they were the most delightful thing he'd seen all day, it was hard not to be awed by him. Not to want to hug him. To feel his arms around her, too.

This was the Simon Purdy she'd hoped would be inside him. Tonight she'd seen the real man. Why on earth was this glorious nurturer standing behind his decision not to embrace life and a family? Yes, he'd lost his wife, but… There had to be another reason she didn't know.

But, again, like his tie, Simon's life wasn't hers to straighten.

None of your business, Isabella.

If she started on trying to convince him she might cry.

Instead, she talked about her family. 'It was good to talk about Gran. Even for a little bit.'

He nodded thoughtfully as he slid into his seat belt and snapped it shut. 'Must have been.'

He tapped his watch. A high-pitched electronic voice said, 'It's eight-fifteen!'

She pushed back in the seat and turned her head briefly. 'What was *that*?'

He laughed. 'Mickey Mouse. The boys love it when I change my watch to Mickey.'

'You have a Mickey Mouse watch?'

'I'm a paediatrician. Of course I do.' He grinned at her amused face. 'I meant to change it back to silent when they went to sleep.'

'You're full of surprises.'

'You have no idea…' He waggled his brows.

'It's still early. Would you like a drink at the hotel bar until you see your father? I can just get an Uber home at nine.'

She'd like that. She wasn't sure how sensible it was, because the way she felt towards Simon Purdy right now she needed to take two steps back before she did more than straighten his tie.

She started the car and drove out of the car park towards the airport.

'Company at the hotel sounds good. If you don't mind? I'd love that. Saves me sitting by myself, watching the clock. You could even come with me to see my father, if you don't want to wait for an Uber. I'll only be there half an hour. If that. I'm sure he'll be interested to hear straight from a paediatrician about his new granddaughter. But he'll be keen to get back to work on his computer.'

'Easily done,' he said, and turned his head briefly to study her face. She felt his gaze on her. 'Barring Henry calling me,' he added.

Oh, heck. She'd forgotten about Henry. About Simon's world. Being on call. She'd lived with being on call with her father. Even been on call herself when she'd worked for retrievals. She remembered how much that impacted on life—more than expected.

That was why she'd gone for an academic, like Conlon. No on call. No emergencies. No need to be constantly aware and ready to go at a moment's notice. Being there when families needed you.

Right… And how had *that* worked out for her?

Not so good. She'd deleted another text from Conlon today without reading it.

'Dad's at the airport hotel. We can park underneath. Apparently, there's a bar on the top floor with excellent views, open till eleven tonight.'

'Perfect. We'll wing it when your father arrives.'

'Was that a pun?'

'I'm a funny guy.' He smiled at her. 'You just haven't met him yet.'

And that was how she found herself on the top floor of a beach-themed hotel, looking over the lights of the Gold Coast with Simon Purdy. On the horizon, the lights of ships glowed as they chugged up and down the coast. Behind them the planes were coming in to land.

Simon put two steaming chai teas down and slung his big frame into the high stool.

'You're buying for me again. Thank you.'

'You're welcome. You've had a big week with your sister. So Kate's the first baby in the family?'

She took a sip of the tea. Hot and soothing. 'My niece? Yes. I've only the one sister. Our mother died when we were young.'

'Like Malachi and me. Both our mothers died early too, and if it wasn't for Millicent, Malachi would have had no warmth in his life at all. That's why Lisandra is such a joy.'

'Makes sense.' Isabella huffed a sad laugh. 'Sounds like my world. My father was too busy for either of us after my mother was gone. If it wasn't for my grandmother…' Her words trailed off as she thought of Gran then and Gran now.

'That must make it doubly hard for you to see her so ill.'

Simon's words were quiet, not over-sentimental. It was as if he knew not to be too sympathetic or she might cry.

The thought eased the tightness in her throat caused by his words.

Isabella lifted her chin and looked at him. 'We went to boarding school, but Gran was the one who took us on holidays. Made sure we knew about cuddles and hugs. She's the person I love most in the world.'

'I bet she has some stories about you.'

Isabella surprised herself when she laughed. He had such a way of lifting her up. 'She does. But what about you? You lost your mother? What was your childhood like?'

His face closed. 'No memories of my mother. She died when I was born. I don't think my father ever forgave me for that.'

CHAPTER SEVENTEEN

SIMON COULD NOT believe he'd just told her his deepest secret. Malachi was the only other person who knew. And probably Lisandra now, because Malachi would keep nothing from his wife.

Hopefully, Isabella would let it go.

'I'm sorry, Simon. Did you have any mother figure who gave you hugs? At least I had Gran.'

He sighed. Nope. She wasn't going to let it go.

'There were housekeepers. My grandmother died not long before my mother.'

'Well, you wouldn't know it from the way you interacted with Malachi's family. You look very balanced.'

'Do I?' He smiled at her. 'Diplomatic… Especially after the way I treated you last week.'

'We'll come to that—but not here. Ah…here comes my father. And soon I'll introduce you to my grandmother.'

'It is unlikely your grandmother will wake, Isabella.'

Simon heard the voice behind his right shoulder. He stood, sliding to the left and moving closer, instinctively, to Isabella, as if to offer her protection from the coldness in the man's words.

Isabella stood up as well. 'Good evening, Dad.' She inclined her head.

There wasn't even a hug between them. It had to be the coldest father-daughter reunion he'd ever seen, and Isabella wasn't a cold woman. He'd known that from the first moment he'd seen her. In fact…

No, he didn't want to go there.

Maybe her dad had realised his lack of warmth would reflect badly, because the man stepped forward and touched Isabella's shoulder. 'I'm aware how fond you are of your grandmother, but you need to be realistic. I spoke to the staff yesterday and there's no change. That's not good.'

Isabella ignored his comment and turned to Simon. 'Dad, I'd like to introduce you to Dr Simon Purdy, a consultant paediatrician where I work. Simon, this is my father, Professor Piers Hargrave, Director of Neurology at Sydney Central.'

Simon put out his hand to the older man and Piers shook it briefly, but Simon was marvelling at the strength and composure in the woman beside him. He could only imagine the distress her father's comments would have caused her. Good grief! Had he heard the man actually say he knew Isabella was *fond* of her grandmother, when anyone could see she adored the woman?

'Are you the consultant for my granddaughter?'

It looked as if Piers Hargraves had finished on the topic of his mother. Maybe that was for the best.

And Simon could do composed, too. 'Yes. Kate

is as stable as any thirty-two-week prem can be. At the moment, we see no reason to expect more complications as she grows. But of course everything is fluid.'

'More complications?'

The question was fired at him.

'She's undergoing phototherapy at the moment. But has successfully commenced EBM through her NG tube. We're pleased that she doesn't require supplemental oxygen or respiratory support now.'

Piers nodded at Simon and then looked at Isabella. 'How's Nadia?'

Nice that he'd asked, thought Simon—but maybe he was doing the man a disservice.

Isabella remained steady. 'We expect her to be discharged from Intensive Care tomorrow morning and transferred to a room near the NICU. Her blood pressure is coming down. It was a rapid onset of eclampsia, as I said on the phone. Dr Madden is the consultant looking after her. He seems happy with her progress. You should call him tomorrow.'

'Excellent. Thank you for the update.' He glanced at his watch. 'I expect to be here until the flight out tomorrow afternoon. I'll see Nadia and…' he hesitated over his granddaughter's name '… Kate.' He looked at Isabella. 'Is that her full name?'

'Yes. Though it is a derivative of Catherine.'

He frowned. 'Right… I imagine I'll see you tomorrow, Isabella?' He inclined his head at Simon. 'Dr Purdy.'

Then he was gone.

Isabella watched him go and then Simon heard her say softly, 'And that stellar conversationalist was my father. All warm and fuzzy, as usual.'

Simon studied the expressionless face beside him and his mouth quirked. 'As you say, I need to meet your grandmother. Because you are nothing like *him*.'

Isabella turned her face to his, and despite the tinge of sadness in her eyes he saw her lips twitch.

'Apparently, I have his brains. But I refused to go into medicine when he wanted me to. Things got even cooler then.'

She looked a little lost, and he didn't want her father to do that to her. 'Nursing's gain and medicine's loss. Now, would you like another drink? Maybe a stiff one? Or would you like to go home?'

She laughed. Which surprised him and possibly her, too.

'Thank you, Simon. For being here.' She raised her brows at him. 'Actually, I'd like to go home and have a stiff drink.'

That was dangerous, but wild horses couldn't drag him away from such an idea.

'Let's do that.'

Isabella drove. He'd opened her door for her,

then strode round to the other side to climb in. Neither had said anything but they'd both smiled.

He watched her handle the car beautifully, slipping through the traffic and down into the parking garage as if the car was on rails. When she'd pulled up they sat there for a few seconds, letting the engine tick as it cooled down.

'Your place or mine?' he said as he looked across at her from the passenger seat. She looked small and tired. And a little bit wounded. Which was a contrast to the confident woman he'd seen in the rooftop bar, talking to her father.

He felt the privilege of her allowing him to see her distress. He didn't want to take advantage. But he also wanted to be there for her. So the dilemma… Too much or too little being there for her? That was why he'd passed the decision to Isabella.

She said quietly, 'I'd like you to come up. To Gran's apartment. With me.'

Simon nodded. 'Stay there,' he said, and slipped out of the car and went around to her side and opened the door.

'You don't have to open my door.'

'It gives me pleasure.'

And it did. He wanted to protect and nurture her, despite the complex, rippling ramifications of that. What he didn't know was what *she* wanted.

She shrugged and slid gracefully from the vehicle. 'Feel free.'

She smiled, and that smile shone a little more vibrantly than before.

Pleased, he walked with her across to the lifts and used his key to let them in. He stretched out his arm across the doors as she stepped through and then followed her.

He could see she wasn't thinking about the present moment, because she didn't even move to the buttons they needed to press.

He pushed seven. The doors closed.

'We've done a lot of lift travelling today, haven't we?'

There's a conversation, he thought. As a starter, it was pretty useless.

But she lifted her head. Glanced his way.

'We have.'

And there was something there, at the back of her voice, that he'd like to know more about. Follow up. Explore…

The lift stopped before either of them said anything else. Again, he put his arm in front of the doors as she walked past to her grandmother's door. Yep. Protective. He could feel his own need. It had started.

She used her key and didn't wait for him. Just left the door open behind her.

Simon followed and closed the door to temptation behind him with a click.

His heart went thump at that same moment.

CHAPTER EIGHTEEN

ISABELLA PUT HER leather clutch down with tingling fingers. Her whole body was warm from standing next to Simon in the lift. She slipped out of the silk jacket she'd had tailored in Vietnam and took it through to the hanger in her wardrobe. The jacket and trousers had been one of those indulgences she'd promised herself.

Tonight, she'd dressed for dinner with friends, but the choice of outfit had been for her father more than Simon. Really it had. Of course, dear Dad hadn't noticed or commented on it. Though, she could tell Simon had admired it.

When she came back into the sitting room Simon still lounged against the door. Waiting for permission to enter further?

He said softly, 'You looked stunning tonight.'

It was as if he'd heard her thoughts. But he couldn't have.

'You still look stunning. That colour is amazing on you. I've never seen anything quite like it.'

The way he'd said *'never seen'* was almost as if he meant he'd never seen anything quite like *her*. And it was a very nice balm for her apparent insignificance to her father.

She rubbed her arms, because the warmth increased and suddenly her skin felt super-charged as he looked at her.

She could almost hear Gran scolding her for feeling slighted by her dad. *'Drama, drama, drama!'*

She tried to let it go. Gran had also said, *'Thank someone if they pay you a compliment.'*

'Thank you, Simon.'

She waved him to the little bar in the corner, where the sherry and the spirits lived.

Obediently, he shifted. As she watched his muscular body ease into motion, calm and unhurried, yet eating the distance from the door, that slow, primitive warmth settled low in her belly.

Oh my. There goes a man who could help a person forget anything.

She'd enjoyed the intimate side of her relationship with Conlon, but she'd never felt this heat Simon generated just by standing there in front of her. This awareness. This lust that was coiling deep inside. Yes, Simon had annoyed and frustrated her before yesterday, but she'd always been aware of her overwhelming physical attraction to him. After tonight at the Maddens' it was more than physical. It was a little too close to consuming.

As if he'd picked up on her thoughts, his voice sounded deeper than usual when he asked, 'What's your definition of a stiff drink?'

She felt the timbre of his quiet words slide into her bones. *Oh my.* She should *not* be going down this path.

'Gran has a lovely cognac...'

It was as if they were both playing a part in a play. Pretending to be normal.

Then she thought of her father's comment.

'I'll replace it when she comes home.'

She heard the harshness in her tone when she said that. But, damn it, her father was wrong.

'As I said before,' Simon murmured as he poured, 'I can't wait to meet Catherine.'

Isabella crossed the room. Simon still had his back to her as he poured the drinks, and she gave in to the urge to slip her arms around his waist and rest her cheek against his broad back, looking for the comfort she knew she'd find there.

He was warm—hot, really—and muscularly hard. He smelled like cinnamon and the wind out on the ocean.

She closed her eyes and breathed him in. Letting go of the tension that had risen higher every day and coiled deep inside her, with Gran not waking, her sister's crisis, Kate's frailty, and tonight waiting for her father.

'Thank you, Simon. Thank you for being with me tonight. Thank you for being there during that incredibly painful five minutes my father could spare me. Thank you for understanding that I need to hope Gran will be back here.'

He put the crystal glasses down on the silver tray with a gentle *ting* that seemed to shimmer in the air like the sound of Tibetan bowls.

Very, very slowly, he unfastened her hands from around his waist, slid them to hold in his, and turned to look down on her so that the front of her body lay against his chest. He studied her face and then leaned down and kissed her lips gently, until he pulled back to stare at the spot he'd just saluted.

His gaze darkened to midnight-blue as it met her eyes. Her heart tripped. She could still feel the imprint of his mouth, hot against hers, and taste the chai on his breath.

In that deep gravelly voice that sent tingles through her, he said, 'You, dear Isabella, are very welcome.'

She loved the way he said her name. And he didn't step back. Didn't let her go. Didn't push on.

All it would take was one lift of her chin up to his mouth and she could forget. Escape from so much. Lose herself in Simon Purdy until tomorrow. She searched his eyes, but he wasn't giving her any pressure. This was her decision.

And what of tomorrow? What then? What of now? What about her needs? The comfort she needed right at this moment? Had needed since she'd landed in Australia?

Simon was offering that. *Simon.* He'd already

said it wasn't a relationship thing. But he would be gentle and kind and most likely a wonderful lover.

And tonight she'd feel warm and cared-for.

She searched his face. What if Simon needed it too? How long since he'd felt cared-for? She suspected it had been far too long.

With that thought she lifted her mouth to his.

Thankfully, he didn't need to be told twice.

Simon's strong hand lifted to her neck and he tilted her head back to expose her throat. His fingers slid down her cheek, down her throat, past the side of her breast and down to the small of her back in a hot trail, coming to rest just above the crease of her buttocks.

He pulled her in against him. Gently, but firmly. He was interested, too. Very interested.

'You taste like chai and sunshine,' he murmured into her hair.

'You taste like chai and the waves out on the beach.'

'Just one night…' he murmured against her mouth as he tilted his face down at her. 'I need you to know it's just one night.'

She stared into the depths of his eyes. Saw the fear in his. The need for mutual comfort.

'One night, or one night at a time,' she breathed. 'Either is fine.'

The hand that rested in the small of her back slid down until he caught her under the swell of her hips and swept her up against his chest.

'Lucky it's Saturday tomorrow and I'm not on duty till the afternoon,' he said. 'Because I'm planning on a late night.'

CHAPTER NINETEEN

DECIDING TO SPEND the night with Simon was like surfing the first wave she'd ever ridden.

A leap of faith that she wouldn't fall flat on her face and get hurt.

And, like that first exhilarating wave, carnal pleasure with Simon had been everything she'd hoped for and more as she'd lifted her face to the sky and flew.

It had turned out to be a mutual delight and an unexpected healing. But both of them knew it wasn't happily-ever-after.

Now it was morning. The pillow was cold beside her. Like the space under her ribs as she realised he wasn't there and she didn't know why. He'd said one night but she'd not even had that. Just hours. And then he'd left.

In the early hours she'd dropped into a boneless sleep in his arms. It must have been some time after that when he'd slipped away. Had he left to avoid talking when they woke? Had she not been good enough? Or had he been called out?

This was why she didn't have one-night stands.

How had this seemed like a good idea last night?

For pity's sake. She had to work this afternoon and face the man.

What she needed was the fresh start of the ocean, but she wasn't sure she wanted to meet Simon face to face in the waves either.

His pique at her invading his surf-space suddenly became more understandable.

But maybe that was the best place to meet him. Floating on a board. A distance apart. With the excuse of looking forward as well as behind them to see a promising wave.

So that was what she did.

The sand flew cold and grainy from her bare feet as she ran towards the breakers. The seagulls were squawking, as if they knew there was juicy gossip to be had, and she squinted up at them balefully.

'Go eat a chip.'

She'd been avoiding it, but now, as she drew closer, Isabella narrowed her gaze to the waves. The space where Simon had been last time and she hadn't recognised his face.

Well, that wasn't going to happen now. She'd identify him, all right.

She'd traced the lines of his cheekbones. And his mouth. *Oh my....* That mouth could do wonderful things. She'd gripped the hard muscles of his body and…

Nope. No forgetting Simon Purdy—today or probably ever.

Her cheeks warmed even with the cool breeze

on them, but her lips curved as the water sloshed up her ankles and knees and she jogged into the waves. Leaning down, she pushed the surfboard in front of her and launched herself along it, to push the water past with her hands.

Her breath caught as she saw a lone figure ahead. She wondered what time he'd come out. Because he was just sitting there. Like a lone pirate surveying the world. Now he was surveying her.

She paddled towards him, but not too close, always leaving a distance between their boards.

'Good morning, Dr Purdy,' she called as she sat up on her fibreglass island.

'Good morning, Isabella. A beautiful morning.'

But there was more in his voice than a remark on the weather, and his blue, blue eyes were looking at her as if she was the best thing he'd seen since he got here.

Her cheeks heated again, and she glanced away from him to the horizon, and the movement of water towards them.

She gestured with her arm. 'Nice swells coming in. Had some good rides?'

She did not just say that. *Shoot.* Her face scorched this time, and she spluttered and shut her mouth.

Simon was too much of a gentleman to laugh, but his eyes danced.

She turned her back on him, paddled quickly,

and caught a wave, even though it wasn't as perfect as she would have normally chosen. Right now she needed space.

Surprisingly, considering the mediocrity of the ride, Simon followed her. When she slipped off the back of the wave he paddled strongly towards her, white teeth gleaming, all rippling muscles, brown skin and big arms bringing him closer.

When he'd closed the distance he paddled up beside her and murmured, 'We said it wasn't going to be awkward.'

'It's not,' she lied.

He raised his brows at her. 'Do you regret spending the night with me?'

She looked up then, and forced herself to hold his gaze. 'Do you with me?'

He laughed. 'No, gorgeous. How could I? You were amazing.'

Oh. That was all right, then.

A weight fell off her shoulders.

'Then, no. You were pretty wonderful, too.'

And suddenly the awkwardness between them slipped into the water beneath them and she smiled.

His teeth gleamed again. 'Although perhaps what we shared last night could be a little more distracting than either of us expected.'

'Sorry.'

My word, it was certainly distracting.

'I'm not much of an expert at morning-afters.' She put her head down, suddenly shy.

She heard his voice, but she still wasn't looking at him as they paddled side by side, up and over another wave.

'Surprisingly, neither am I. Henry rang me not long after you went to sleep. I left to speak to him.'

Isabella sucked in a breath.

He held up his hand. 'Not about Kate. Your niece is fine.'

And that allayed two concerns in one. He hadn't left because of any awkwardness or because he was uncaring. He'd left for work. And he'd reassured her about Kate before she could jump to wrong conclusions.

'Thank you, Simon. You're a thoughtful man.' She lifted her head and risked looking into his face. 'Race you to the back?'

When they'd surfed the early morning away, they stopped at Lulu's café for breakfast.

As Simon was off duty, and Isabella was not working until the afternoon, they had time—unless their phones rang.

Lulu swept up, pencil behind her ear and notepad in her hand, her usual exuberant self. 'Good morning, you two. How's the surf?'

'Nice swells, thanks, Lulu.'

Simon leaned back in his chair and Isabella tried not to stare at his strong throat and chest above the open neck of his shirt. It was as if everything about him had taken on colour and tactile recognition and scent and memory, but he was still talking to Lulu.

'How're the twins?'

'Full of mischief. The usual for you, Simon? And what about you, Isabella? Smashed avocado and eggs on rye? Orange juice and coffee?

Isabella smiled up at the woman. She'd remembered her name and her previous order. 'Great memory, Lulu. All of the above, but a skinny cap, please.'

'Done.' Lulu swung away with her notebook.

'Why does she carry a notebook if she remembers everything?'

'For the chef. I've seen Lulu take an order from ten people at a table and bring out the correct food to everybody without writing a thing down. That's her superpower.'

'I think her personality is her superpower. She's amazing.'

Simon was looking at her with a smile on his face.

'What?' she asked.

'Some people might judge her for the piercings and the tattoos.'

'She's vibrant and happy and amazing. All the while loving twin babies. No judgement.' Isabella shrugged. 'So, what was the problem in the unit last night?'

She could do this. Talk to Simon normally after a night of incredible, bone-melting… She didn't like to call it sex. It had been more than that. How about mutual appreciation? Tenderness? Gentleness? A little bit of wildness. And lots of healing. She felt as if every knot in her body had been undone.

'Earth to Isabella?' Simon was watching her face and his blue eyes had darkened to ocean-depth-blue. 'You might want to stop looking at me like that…'

Her face flushed. Her neck heated. She closed and opened her eyes. 'Oh, dear.' She raised her gaze to his face. 'This is your fault.'

He laughed. 'I am not taking all the blame. No way. And last night at work it was the new twins.'

Lulu brought their coffee and juice and put their cups down. She didn't say anything, but she waved her hand at her own face as if fanning it. The smile in her eyes said, *It's smokin' hot over here!*

Once Lulu was gone, Isabella said quietly, 'So where do we go from here, Simon?'

'I'll go back home. I imagine you'll visit your grandmother, get ready for work, and visit your sister before you start. And I'll run into you this afternoon in the unit. At least we have two days before Carla is back with her eagle eyes, ready to tease us. Everything will be fine by then.'

She wondered if he really would *imagine*, daydream, or think about her while she was doing all that.

'You have experience in all this,' she accused.

He'd just laid out a very sensible plan, but it was sweet that he'd paid enough attention to know what her movements would be.

CHAPTER TWENTY

SIMON WASN'T EXPERIENCED. Not with what had happened last night. He'd played around a bit before he'd met Louise, but since her death he'd been in cold storage. Now Isabella Hargraves had swooped in, and lust had taken him by dangerous and heated surprise.

Last night, while incredible, had been so momentous he knew without a doubt it had been a mistake. No way could he do that again and walk away.

Not with how amazing it had been and how hazardous it was to his resolution to stay single and safe from the type of pain he couldn't even contemplate going through again.

Isabella would want it all. She deserved it all. He just couldn't give it to her. He couldn't keep her safe.

He would remain focused on his career. He would not go down the route of falling in love.

Isabella Hargraves had all the makings of an addiction. And he knew where that led.

A place he wasn't going. Hadn't he told himself that before? Didn't matter. It had never been as important to remember as it was this morning.

They would finish breakfast and go their separate ways. And when they met in the unit he would be pleasantly friendly, because she deserved that. But he would pretend nothing had happened.

Eventually, she'd get it. He hoped.

Except he was kidding himself.

Simon grimaced into his coffee and pushed that thought away along with the cup.

The food arrived and they both tucked in.

It seemed neither of them had eaten for a week, because there was no word said as they shovelled the nourishment down. He hadn't been this hungry for years. Three years, in fact.

They sat back at the same time and looked at each other, and then looked down at their empty plates. And he couldn't help it. He laughed when she did.

'Apparently surfing works up an appetite,' he said.

She pushed her gorgeous lips together, as if holding words back, and he just knew what she was going to say.

Surfing wasn't the only thing that had given them an appetite.

He needed to run away. Tried to say, *I have to go.*

The one time he wanted his phone to ring and it wouldn't do it!

His phone rang.

Thank you, heaven.

His pulse rate settled.

There we go.

He stood up.

She said thoughtfully, studying his face, 'I'll pay for this. You go.'

And, contrarily, just for a moment he didn't want to leave.

CHAPTER TWENTY-ONE

THAT. THERE. THE TWITCH. The flicker she'd seen in his eyes. He'd wanted to get away, to get to work. That was her father all over again. She felt the knowledge slide in, felt as if she'd been stabbed with one of the happy, beachy purple knives off the table, straight in her heart.

Simon wanted to leave her behind and get on with more exciting business-like work.

It stung. She'd told herself that she was fine for a one-night stand. And on one hand it had been a good decision to sleep with Simon—apart from all the benefits of the best sex she'd ever had—because now she knew, without investing in any more wishy-washy thoughts of the future. Even after what they'd shared, Simon wanted work more than he wanted her!

Message received.

Isabella watched as Simon ate up the distance to the apartments in big strides, even more quickly than if he'd run. And, yes, it all underlined the fact he wanted to get away.

'He's a nice guy,' Lulu said at her shoulder.

'Wonderful.' Isabella sighed and finished her coffee. 'But married to his work. I had a childhood like that. Not doing that for the rest of my life.'

She wasn't sure why she'd told Lulu that, except

Isabella needed to hear it out loud. Her statement solidified in her mind as she reached for her purse.

'And it's grateful I am that he is,' Lulu murmured, and there was emotion and a hint of Irish brogue under that sentence.

She got that. Oh, yes, Dr Simon Purdy was great at his job. And right now she was glad of that too. She had a niece who needed him.

'Hello, Gran. It's Isabella. I've brought you flowers. Deep purple with a subtle perfume.'

She subconsciously waited for a greeting that never came. Shook her head at herself.

'Violets. Your favourite. That's right…'

She tucked the small vase next to her grandmother on the side table and tweaked one of the blooms more upright.

'They say gently stimulating the five senses might help you to wake up.'

Please, Gran, she thought as emotion clogged. She swallowed the lump in her throat.

'It's four weeks now, so that's enough of this sleeping for you.'

She pulled open the bedside drawer and took out the hand cream. She sat down and picked up her grandmother's thin, wrinkled hand in hers.

'Anyway, back to the five senses. I'm trying to stimulate your hearing, not drive you mad with my babble. And later your friend Millicent is coming to chat as well. Would you like that?'

That made her think about Simon.

She glanced across at her grandmother's face and for a moment she'd thought her eyes were open. They weren't. Her heart thumped faster and then settled down.

Wishful thinking.

Her brain wasn't working properly with images of Simon intruding with every second thought. She'd have to do something about that.

'The flowers are to stimulate your sense of smell…'

She began to smooth the cream into her grandmother's soft hands.

'And I'll spend a little time rubbing your fingers to stimulate your sense of touch.'

With a hint of asperity that wasn't solely directed at her grandmother, thanks to her father and Simon, she said, 'It's a beautiful day outside and you need to wake up.'

There was so much she wanted to tell her grandmother. Wanted to pour out into her ears.

But she was not going to talk about Simon. All she said was, 'The nurse said Dad has been in to see you. Did you recognise his voice?'

When Isabella walked into the neonatal intensive care unit the first person she saw, for a change, was her father. Tall and strangely gaunt-looking, and almost seeming old. She hadn't noticed that last night.

The second person was Simon, too darned handsome and full of stamina, standing beside him, talking beside Kate's cot.

Two tall men. One dark-haired, one light-haired. Both standing there with that consultant doctor attitude. An *I've studied a long time to be able to help this sick patient* look on their faces. Both married to their work. Both saving the world.

Blow the both of them.

She was early, so she had time to have a quick word before she officially started.

She put her bag away in the small staff room and crossed the room towards them.

They stopped talking as she approached. 'Hello, Dad. Simon…' She addressed her father. 'You went to see Gran? What did you think?'

She suspected he wouldn't even have said anything if she hadn't asked.

Her father's cool gaze held a hint of concern, which wasn't like him, and she focussed her attention on him while her stomach dived.

'There's a possibility she's not as deeply unconscious as she has been earlier, but I hesitate to give you false hope. Extensive brain damage is likely.'

And there it was. Did the man not have any heart?

Simon's gaze raked her face and she felt his sympathy. She didn't need it. She was becoming even more disenchanted with her father.

She narrowed her eyes at him. 'Thanks. Don't hold back. I need all the hope I can get.'

She turned to Simon before she said something she'd regret. Her voice softened and she searched his face. 'How's Kate?'

That was the question for now.

She plastered on a cool, calm expression for all to see. She looked down at her sleeping niece and asked, 'All going well?'

Simon spoke quietly. 'Kate's temperature control is erratic. We've had a couple of bradycardias and two occasions of apnoea. We've stopped the feeds for the time being.'

Stopped the feeds? Her stomach plummeted.

'Infection?' That was the most common cause of problems with premature babies. 'Her breathing?' She was certainly breathing a little faster. 'Not NEC…?'

Her brain rifled through the options. Infection they could treat with antibiotics. Kate had already been started on some. Could be anything. Worst-case scenario it could be the beginning of a Necrotising Enterocolitis, but it was very early.

She studied Kate's belly. Was the tiny tummy a little more bloated? It was the third day. That was a horrifying concept.

Simon studied her face as if he could see the thoughts chasing through her mind. 'There is some decrease in bowel sounds,' he said.

She nodded. Ignored her father. Fished her

stethoscope from her pocket, where she kept it to keep it warm, and wiped the membrane and casing—the listening end—with an alcohol swab from her other pocket. When she was done with meticulously cleaning it, she looked for somewhere to put the discarded swab and debris.

Simon held out his hand. Their eyes met and she saw the understanding in his. She settled the wrappings carefully in his palm, as if doing so equalled crossing her fingers behind her back and therefore she could keep Kate safe.

'Thank you,' she murmured, before leaning down to very gently put the stethoscope on Kate's belly to listen. She was hoping Kate's belly would gurgle. Or hiss. All she got was a tiny trickle. The rest was…silence.

She took the stethoscope away. Fear clutched her throat but she pushed it down.

'Do you think her abdomen is swollen?' At Simon's nod she asked quietly, 'How's the gastric aspirate trending? Has it increased?'

'Five mils removed last time.'

'X-ray?'

His intent gaze never left her face. 'There is a small collection of gases.'

'Treatment?'

'Change antibiotics. Nil by mouth for three days and fingers crossed.'

Okay. Standard protocol.

'When did you first notice it?'

'On my round an hour ago.'

He'd called over a radiologist for the X-ray. No doubt he would have ordered blood tests as well.

Pre-empting her question, Simon added, 'Blood results aren't back yet. Not even the preliminary ones.'

Simon was worried—which meant she was worried.

She glanced towards the nurses' station and the staff who had gathered there. 'I'll take the handover report and come back.'

She didn't say it, but she wanted him still to be there. She glanced at her father, but uncharacteristically he didn't say anything. She nodded and left.

CHAPTER TWENTY-TWO

PIERS HARGRAVES SAID, 'My daughter was always very quick on the uptake.'

Simon heard the pride in his voice. And he guessed that he, himself, was a little impressed that he hadn't been wrong about Isabella's ability to take in the situation instantly.

'She could have been a doctor, you know. She chose midwifery.'

Simon heard the curl of disgust in her father's voice. He was liking this guy less and less.

He lifted his chin and met the man's eyes. 'I have no doubt she's an amazing midwife. She's certainly brilliant as a neonatal intensivist. We're very lucky to have her.'

'Yes, you are. Hopefully she won't stay. I'm keen for her to move back to Sydney.'

Simon hoped Isabella's father didn't mean after Piers's mother had passed away. That was just too cold.

Either way, he couldn't see Isabella leaving. Not with Nadia here. And Kate. Even though Kate's situation was worrisome, Simon was quietly confident the baby would rise to the challenge. He thought this would only be a small setback, because they'd hit the problem quickly.

No doubt Isabella would think that too.

But he wasn't saying that out loud. He wasn't going to guarantee anything or make promises he couldn't keep.

And that went for other things as well. No promises anywhere about anything.

But was that just like Isabella's father?

Simon changed the subject. 'How's Nadia?' He hadn't seen Kate's mother today though he planned to go there now. Now that he'd seen Isabella.

'The oedema is receding. And her blood pressure is stable. It appears there is no sequalae. She's said she'll try to walk to the NICU late this afternoon.'

'Of course. I imagine she's been waiting for Isabella's shift. I'll ask them to bring her in a wheelchair.'

Piers dropped his voice. 'What is your intention with my daughter?'

Simon almost said *Nadia?* just to annoy him. But he didn't. And as for Isabella… He wished he knew.

'We have a mutual respect,' he said gravely. And left it at that.

Anything else was not her father's business—especially after the cold way he'd treated his daughter in the bar at that airport hotel.

Simon didn't want to think about why he was feeling so protective.

He saw the good doctor glance across at the

nurses circumnavigating the unit, stopping at each cot to discuss progress and treatment. He glanced at his watch.

Surely Piers wouldn't…?

'Let's go over and you can say goodbye. That'll be better than just slipping away. She's finding it tough,' Simon said, pre-empting Isabella's father's obvious intention of getting Simon to pass on a farewell message. Words that might sting Isabella with dismissal.

No. Simon wasn't going to let him do it.

He turned and crossed the room, and guided Piers to where the nurses were gathered to discuss their next patient.

'Sorry for the interruption, ladies,' Simon said. 'Isabella?' She looked at him. 'Could I borrow you for a moment, please?'

Seeing as he tended to do that all the time, nobody was surprised.

She detached herself and came to where he'd moved, back to Piers's side.

Her father's lips were pressed together. 'Goodbye, Isabella. You're doing a good thing, being here for Nadia. For everyone. Thank you.'

Simon saw her surprise and the quickly veiled pleasure at her father's words and breathed out a little deeper in relief, fiercely glad he'd leant on the other man to make a formal goodbye.

'Thank you,' she said quietly, and leaned forward to kiss his cheek. 'Safe flight.'

Her father nodded and strode away.

Simon saw the questioning look in her eyes. 'Yes. I'll still be here when you finish.'

It was her turn to nod, but he saw that same satisfaction flare briefly, and his own pleasure at her response sat warm in his chest.

'Thank you.'

She turned and walked back to the group and he went to the desk to call Pathology, to see if any results had come through for Kate.

CHAPTER TWENTY-THREE

IN THE END, just before tea, Simon went to the post-natal ward and brought Nadia back in a wheelchair himself, to sit beside Kate.

Isabella didn't know what he'd said to her, but Nadia looked calm and composed, and she understood that her baby had issues that needed dealing with.

For Isabella, her concern was shelved as she watched her sister reach out and touch her daughter's hand for the first time. A baby too sick to travel up to visit and a mother to unstable to be transported down from the intensive care. But Nadia was in the new room on the same floor now. Everything would be easier. That small, tentative mother's touch brought tears to Isabella's eyes.

Hospital policy made it against the rules for its staff to care for their own relatives, so Isabella wasn't looking after Kate. But while she was not responsible for her care or observations, she could—and did—keep an eye on her from her side of the unit.

Thankfully, it seemed a quieter afternoon in the unit. Nice, Isabella thought, because it meant she could slip over and talk to her sister when she had questions. Also, it would be her break time soon, and she would spend it with Nadia.

Simon had disappeared to the emergency department, to treat a three-year-old girl with epilepsy, but had promised to come back.

Her sensible brain would have preferred he went home and got some sleep, just in case he was needed for her niece…

'Has Dad gone?' asked Nadia, glancing at her watch.

Nadia. Think about Nadia. Be present.

'Yes, he left not long after I started shift. I guess that means he didn't drop in to see you on his way out?'

Nadia shook her head and Isabella could see the quickly veiled hurt.

Darn him, Isabella seethed. What would it have cost him? Three minutes? Nadia was five doors away from the NICU.

'He said he was going to see Gran today, but he didn't come back to tell me what he thought about her prognosis.'

Isabel wanted to grind her teeth. The man had real issues with being a parent, and for the first time she wondered how many times her grandmother had actually forced him to do things that they'd thought he'd instigated himself.

'Did he tell *you* how Gran was?' Nadia asked.

Isabella said gently, 'He said he thought she wasn't as deeply unconscious as before, but he's not optimistic.'

She didn't say that she'd thought their grandmother's eyes had opened. Or that their father thought brain damage would be a problem.

'Imagine that…' Nadia drawled grimly. 'Dad not being optimistic…' She glanced up at Isabella, said softly, 'I'm sorry I didn't go more often to see her before Kate was born. It just upset me too much.'

Isabella leant down and hugged her. 'It's okay. I understand. Being pregnant mucks with your emotions.'

Right then Kate's cardiac monitor alarm went off, and Isabella watched the screen as her niece's heart rate slowly dropped. She glanced across to the nurse looking after her, who nodded and slipped across to watch as well.

Isabella said softly in Nadia's ear, 'We don't want to stimulate her—we want her to stimulate herself. But we will if her lack of breath and falling heart rate goes on for longer than thirty seconds.'

Nadia paled, and Isabella squeezed her sister's shoulder.

After seventeen seconds Kate breathed in, and her cardiac output increased as her heart rate went back up.

'Good girl,' Isabella said, and the nurse next to them smiled.

'She didn't need stimulation,' the nurse explained to Nadia. 'She's managing.'

'Yes, thanks… I see,' said Nadia, but her eyes

tracked back to Isabella, who nodded encouragingly.

'Jesse has this. She'll watch her,' Isabella said, and then continued, 'I'd better get back to my own babies. See you soon. Let me know when you want to go back to bed.'

Nadia nodded unhappily. 'I'll stay another ten minutes, but I'm getting sore…'

Isabella frowned. 'If you're in pain, only stay a few minutes more, while I phone an orderly to take you back to your ward. I'll come and see you in your room when I go on my next break.'

Forty minutes later, after all her babies were fed and their observations were up to date, Isabella went along to Nadia's room with the packed dinner she'd brought from home.

Nadia was just finishing off her own tray of food.

Nadia's first words—'Kate's good?'—made Isabella smile.

'Kate's good.'

'Great. And now, because I'm dying to know…' Her sister sat back expectantly. 'How was your date at Dr Madden's house with the hunky Dr Purdy?

Isabella smiled. Her sister had been very patient. 'Hunky Dr Purdy, eh?'

She was thankful this conversation hadn't come up on the unit, with everyone within earshot.

'Not my type.' Nadia tilted her head. 'But definitely hunky.'

She looked crestfallen for a second, and Isabella guessed Nadia had just remembered her late husband. The man had been not a happy partner in life for Nadia. A gambler and unfaithful. It would take time, and someone very special, for Nadia to trust a man again. Her sister did not need to go there yet, and Isabella could sacrifice a little privacy to cheer her up.

'It was fun,' she said, pretending she hadn't seen Nadia's punctured mood. 'And Lisandra Madden is a lovely woman I hope I see more of.'

'That's nice…' Nadia surreptitiously wiped her eyes.

'Yes. And I even met Dr Madden's grandmother. Millicent. She's a friend of Gran's.'

Nadia opened her eyes wide. 'Is she?' She smiled and shook her head. 'It's like a small town here.'

Isabella laughed. 'Probably because we're all connected through the hospital. Anyway, it was a lovely dinner, great conversation, and Lisandra's twins are gorgeous.'

'I'm jealous.' Nadia sounded wistful. 'You're making new friends and I haven't made any.'

Isabella opened the tucker box on her lap. 'It will happen.' She popped a cherry tomato into her mouth.

'But what about Simon?' Her sister shifted on

her pillows as if trying to get comfortable. 'Did he kiss you goodnight?'

Isabella's mind flew back to that long look in the lounge room of Gran's apartment, and the way, after that, Simon had carried her to bed. She slowed her chewing to give herself time to answer.

My word, he'd kissed her.

Her stomach curled, kicked and rolled.

She looked down at her food box.

He'd kissed her so many times. In so many places. She didn't think she'd ever forget that night. Or his mouth…

Instead of answering the question, and fighting down the heat that wanted to flood her cheeks, she offered, 'Simon and I called into the airport hotel after we left. He even came with me when I spoke to Dad. He met us in the bar.'

Nadia opened her eyes wide. 'Did he?' Thankfully she was diverted. 'That's above and beyond for Simon.' Then she frowned. 'How did Dad take that?'

'Didn't blink an eye.' Isabella grimaced. 'But then it didn't take very long. I was out of there in five minutes.'

Nadia shook her head. 'What do you think is wrong with our father? Do you think we'll be like that when we're old?'

Isabella couldn't help but laugh. 'He's not old. But no, I'm not turning into an antisocial pessimist. I refuse. And neither will you. I'm starting to think Gran is the only reason we're both turned out so well.'

That brought the mood down again. They were both thinking about Gran, lying there unconscious, her eyes closed. Not what she'd intended. But at least it diverted Nadia from asking about Simon kissing her goodnight again.

'Do you think she'll wake up?' asked Nadia.

'Yes. I do. When she's ready.'

Strangely, her dwindling hope had taken off again.

Isabella took a bite of her sandwich, because she needed to eat before she went back to work and she only had fifteen minutes left.

'Did you see Dr Madden today? Sorry I haven't asked before.'

Nadia nodded. 'Yes, just before lunch. He says I'm making good progress, but they need to keep checking my blood pressure.'

'I think you're in the golden light of Simon and Malachi now.'

And because that wasn't a bad place to be from Nadia's point of view, she smiled. Nadia and Kate needed the care.

'Also, it's great that we live close for later, as Kate grows up.'

Nadia sighed, long and loud, and then held her aching stomach. 'How long do you think Kate will be in hospital?'

That was the question most asked by parents in

the NICU, Isabella thought, and her sister was no different. 'I always tell people that however early the baby is in weeks is the general length of time they're going to stay in hospital.

'It could be eight weeks?' Nadia sounded forlorn.

'Could be... But probably closer to five. There'll be ups and downs, like today, so it's hard to tell.'

She pointed her finger at Nadia. 'But her mother and her auntie will be here for as long as it takes, and the time will pass. She just needs to be well and grow up. It will happen.'

CHAPTER TWENTY-FOUR

SIMON DROPPED BACK into the NICU after the emergency department's call, hoping to catch Isabella before he went home. He'd planned to give her the pathology results personally, but she wasn't there.

He knew where she'd be.

On her break with her sister. Caring.

He should go home. The result would be in Kate's records soon, and the staff would let Isabella know when she came back. That would be in less than half an hour. He didn't need to go looking for her all over the hospital.

Except his feet carried him out of the NICU and along the corridor to the postnatal area and Nadia's room. He could hear Isabella's voice as he approached.

'It will happen.'

What will happen?

He couldn't help thinking of last night, and paused at the door to gather himself as memories tried to break through the wall he'd erected. Yes, it had happened. He squeezed his eyes shut, trying to hold back the images.

My word, it had.

He knocked. Two blonde heads turned his way, and two pairs of green eyes: one pair sleepy and owl-like because of the drugs, and the other alert, cool, and too beautiful for their own good. How did he find one of these sisters totally pole-axing and the other merely pleasant? Nadia was a beautiful woman, too, but Isabella stole his breath.

'Pathology back?' Isabella said softly as her brows rose in question.

He hadn't really noticed people's brows before, but hers were arched, darker than her hair. They drew the eye to the angles of her face. Perfect.

What was he doing? Spending seconds he didn't need to thinking thoughts he shouldn't be thinking. He should be walking in the opposite direction. Jogging? Sprinting?

The thought soured in his mind, and he pushed it away.

'Pathology? Yes. Not looking too bad. If Kate has an inflamed bowel, it's only just started, and hopefully the antibiotics will stop any spread of infection. We'll keep her nil by mouth and wait. She'll get IV nutrition.'

'Thanks, Simon.' Isabella smiled at her sister. 'That's good news, Nadia.'

Nadia breathed out a sigh. 'Wonderful. So, when will her tummy work again? Should I carry on expressing breast milk?'

He watched Isabella tweak the covers straight on her sister's bed, making sure she was snuggled in.

'You keep expressing every few hours, like you have been. We'll store the milk. There won't be much at first, but it will meet Kate's needs when she's ready. We'll sort that.' Isabella glanced at her watch. 'Thanks for the update, Simon. You going home now?'

He felt dismissed. Maybe she did have a bit of the old man in her. The thought made his mouth twitch. Isabella was nothing like her cold father.

'Yes.' He had a sudden uneasy thought. 'Did you bring your car? How do you normally get home at night after a late shift?'

He walked the block and a half home at night. The fresh air after the air-conditioned hospital felt good. But he didn't like the idea of Isabella out at eleven p.m., when her shift ended, which coincidentally was not long after the pubs shut with all the drunks and revellers emptied onto the streets.

It was dark on the road towards their apartments, even with the streetlights.

'I walk fast,' she said. 'Like you do. And I carry an alarm.'

He opened his mouth and closed it again. Fair enough. Except he wasn't happy. His neck crawled with how unhappy he was.

'She has a black belt in karate,' Nadia said with a wicked, sisterly grin. 'Which she doesn't tell anybody about.'

That made him blink. Why was he surprised? Why did that make her even hotter?

'I should ask you to walk *me* home, then,' Simon quipped, but his brain spun with relief…

and maybe some graphic imaginings of Isabella flying through the air or kicking out at an assailant.

His body stirred. *Hot, or what?*

Nope. Not going there.

It wasn't strange that his mind was on alert—he had feelings for Isabella…complicated feelings. But she was a friend. They'd agreed on that.

Friend with benefits? his libido whispered.

No. No more benefits.

But maybe he'd watch for her out of his balcony tonight and just make sure she was safe.

'I'll leave you, then,' he said, wishing his phone would ring. Why was he still here?

'I'll come with you.' Isabella leaned down to kiss her sister. 'You need sleep, missy. I'm not far away if you need me.'

Ah, Isabella would want to talk to him about the results. That was why he hadn't left. He'd known she'd want that.

It was as if another Simon lived inside him—one tuned to Isabella and Isabella's needs.

He waved, and Isabella said, 'See you tomorrow, Nadia.'

He walked to the door and Isabella followed until they were out in the corridor and halfway back to the NICU. Then she stopped.

'Thanks for being here today, Simon.'

He saw her concern, her worry, and his heart ached a little at the load she carried. But he needed his walls to stay up. Especially when she looked at him like that.

In response, he made light of his part. 'Easy done. I don't have a life.'

That was true. But the statement fell flat. She didn't smile.

'Why is that? Why don't you have a life? You deserve one.'

Her voice was more intense than he'd expected.

His brows furrowed. 'I told you why. I've had my time.'

Because I'm scared that if I allow myself to care and something happens again...

He wasn't going to say that. So he batted the question back to her. 'Why don't *you* have a life, apart from worrying about your family? Where's your home life?'

He hadn't wondered about that before, and suddenly the answer was very, very interesting.

She looked away. Which wasn't like her.

'I tried that in Vietnam. His name was Conlon. He let me down, too.'

He saw the subtle shake of her head, as if she was calling herself a fool for believing in fairy tales. She deserved the fairy tale. He just couldn't give it to her either.

The man must have been a fool. He wanted to say so, because standing there with Isabella he felt as if they were in a bubble, insulated from the world.

Except they weren't alone in the bubble.

An orderly pushed an empty stretcher around the corner and they had to separate to let him through. It broke the spell.

'I'm sorry. It's none of my business. I'd better go.'

Before he said something else stupid.

He turned and left, but he could feel her gaze on him as he walked away.

At ten past eleven that evening Simon stood on his balcony and watched the road between the hospital and the apartments.

He'd never really thought about the fact that he could see his place of work from where he lived, but for the purpose of watching for Isabella it was perfect.

There she was. Right on time. Walking under the first streetlight with a brisk pace and a cross-body bag tucked in front of her. There was something in the droop of her shoulders that said she was unhappy.

He scanned the streets, but there was no one around. Still, he didn't like it. He wanted to slip down in the lift and stand outside, open the door for her.

Crazy on top of crazy. He needed sleep.

He stayed watching.

He'd phoned half an hour ago to check on Isabella's niece, and she'd been stable, so nothing new to worry either of them there. They should both sleep.

But why was she unhappy? Was it him? Had he done this to her?

She must have felt his attention on her, because she glanced up at his balcony and shaded her eyes from the streetlight. He reached his hand back into the apartment and flicked the light on and off.

She offered a tiny wave and he smiled. Felt his whole face crinkle with satisfaction from one miniscule hand lift. *Idiot.*

He texted her. Fingers moving before he could stop them. He hadn't even realised that he had his phone in his hand.

Do you want to come up?

And that was why he was standing there. God, he was such a fool. He hadn't realised that was what he was going to do.

She texted back.

Two minutes.

His libido whispered that he could be fast, if that was what she wanted. Against the door, maybe?

He closed his eyes.

No. No. No. He wasn't going to do this. They weren't going to do this.

He was just there to hear about her night. Be an ear and listen to her, because she didn't have anyone else. Let her unwind so she could sleep without her brain reeling in the night with suppressed conversations she couldn't have on her own.

Like he did. Nearly every night.

He went back inside to the kitchen to put on the kettle. Absently checked there was ice in the freezer in case she wanted something stronger. Put out two mugs. Threw in two sleepy-time teabags.

Because then he wouldn't have to spend time in the kitchen, when really he wanted to look at her, talk to her, not have his back to her making tea.

She knocked at the door before he had time to put everything back and tell himself to stop being stupid, so instead he crossed the room in long strides.

He took a breath to fill his lungs and opened the door, so he could search the features he was coming to know so well.

He'd missed her face.

He frowned when he saw the worry in her eyes. The concern in the pull of her mouth. The weariness. He wanted to hug her.

'Come in,' he said.

She eased past him, bringing the smell of the hospital and handwash in with her.

He shut the door and followed. 'How was your night? I thought you might like a quick debrief before you went to bed.'

Her chin lifted and he saw the glitter of tears. 'Nadia had another seizure. Malachi's with her and she's back in Intensive Care.'

This time he didn't hesitate before he stepped up and pulled her to his chest, wrapping his arms around her. The hug was long and firm. She shuddered with distress under his hands.

'I'm so sorry, Isabella. No wonder you look stressed. I'm glad you came up.'

He tucked his chin on top of her head and breathed in the scent of her hair. Herbs. Flowers. And Isabella.

'What time did it happen?'

'Nine p.m. Malachi came down to see me afterwards. Very kind of him. He said she's stable now, but will have to stay in the ICU for another forty-eight hours at least.'

She lifted the back of her hand to wipe a tear off her cheek.

'I rang Dad. But he was in a late meeting, so I left a message.'

Of course he was. Useless man. Or useless to Isabella, anyway.

She pulled away and he let his arms fall so she could step back.

'Sorry.' She turned her face away. 'You don't need all this drama.'

'Hey…' He lifted a finger and turned her chin back. 'You're the lone lighthouse here, for all these people. It's tough being you. You just keep on being an incredible rock for everyone and I'll help hold up the foundations when you need it.'

She sniffed and lifted her chin, but her mouth trembled. 'I don't feel very rock-like at the moment.'

'How about you roll your rock my way?' He patted his chest. 'Let me be a refuge you can come to when you need it.' He stepped closer and pulled her in again. 'Another hug won't hurt.'

She let him, but she mumbled against his chest, her words vibrating between them.

'You couldn't wait to get away this morning,' she said.

And, yes, he had wanted to get away. He'd actually bolted. And he was ashamed of that. Yet, strangely, he didn't want to escape at this moment.

'But not now,' he said by way of apology.

Because she needed him now. And he couldn't dispute the fact that he needed to be there for her.

'Doesn't mean we're not friends. Just means I'm trying not to promise something I don't think I can give.' He dropped a kiss on her hair. 'But this is now. I can give this. The other is for the future. Would you like a sleepy time tea? Or something stronger?'

She stepped back again. When she looked up at him her mouth had firmed and her eyes were clearer. 'I'll take the tea.'

He nodded and pulled her over to the long sofa

with all the cushions, and made sure she was comfortable before he turned for the kitchen.

He was back less than a minute later, with the tea poured, and a small empty bowl for the tea bag when she was happy with the strength of her beverage.

'Do you need something to eat?'

'I couldn't eat,' she said. 'I've been feeling sick since nine.'

'Understandable. But you know what? Sometimes food helps. How about I make you some cheese on toast cut into soldiers?'

She leaned her head leaned back at that, and stared up at him quizzically.

He shrugged, his face a little warm. 'Malachi made it for me after my wife died and I was doing zombie impersonations. I find it really helps when things get bad.'

She shook her head, as if she couldn't imagine what he described, but then a small smile bloomed on her beautiful mouth. 'Truly, that sounds wonderful. I'd love to try Malachi's soldiers.'

They sat together for the next half an hour, munching on crunchy toast and melted cheese, and drinking sleepy time tea as the clock ticked towards midnight. He'd dimmed the lights, so they could see out through the door towards the twinkling lights of Surfers Paradise across the wide bay.

Outside, the sound of the waves on the beach

made a rhythmic hum as the traffic died away. His arm lay across her shoulders, pulling her into him, and her skin was like silk against his, warm and wonderful. Gradually Isabella relaxed beside him. His own stomach unwound as the tightness in her neck loosened and her head sank back into his arm. Good.

'I checked on Kate at half past ten and everything was fine with her,' Simon murmured quietly, not wanting to upset the mood but giving her the option to talk if she wanted to.

She shifted her head to look at him. She was so close. Kissably close.

'This is nice. I feel better,' she said, off-topic. Then, 'Yes, she looks good. I think you've nailed the danger after that first sign of inflammation. Nipped it in the bud.'

He stared back at her. Her eyes had deepened to emerald in the low light. 'I hope so. When are you on shift again?'

'An evening shift tomorrow.'

He fought with his body to lift his arm from her shoulders, because it really didn't want him to move. 'I, on the other hand, am on duty at eight. And you, missy…' he smiled as he remembered her addressing her sister like that '…need to go to bed.'

And not with me, despite how lovely that would be.

But he didn't say that out loud.

'You need sleep.'

'So do you,' she said. She turned her face and kissed his cheek. 'Thanks for the listening ear. I needed it.'

When she stood, she looked better somehow. Stronger. As if she'd regrouped. And he hoped that he had been a small part of that, even if he couldn't be anything else.

CHAPTER TWENTY-FIVE

ISABELLA'S HEARING SEEMED bizarrely attuned to hear when Simon shut the door after her. But when she got to the lift there had been no sound, and she turned back. He was still waiting.

She furrowed her brows at him. He smiled and waited until she'd slipped inside the elevator and the doors began to close before closing his own door.

That had been lovely interlude after a mad day. Simon had cosseted her. Not something she'd experienced often—someone looking after her.

Gran was bracing. Fun as she was, she expected the girls to look after themselves.

Simon making her cheese on toast soldiers, instead of Isabella doing the nurturing, sat oddly, but was warmly comforting—as it had been intended to be. There was no doubt she felt more serene than she had when she'd walked through Simon's door forty-five minutes ago.

But yes, she was tired. Needed to sleep. And not in Simon's bed. There was no future there. She wasn't going down that rabbit hole before trying to sleep. It would be too easy to get used to it.

The next morning Isabella launched her surfboard into the ocean and let the clarity of the waves wash away the fog, drama and fear of yesterday.

By the time she left the water she felt awake and alive. Ready for the day. Simon wasn't there, though. She'd spent a lot of the time looking. She tried not to worry about Kate just because he was missing. He had promised to call and her waterproof watch said she hadn't missed any attempts of communication.

She jogged back to her apartment with her surfboard under her arm, feeling her body lift and respond as if eager for more of a workout.

Nadia had told Simon about her karate. She hadn't thought about joining a martial arts class up here but that would be a great idea to give her another outlet. A place to stretch her muscles, keep fit and expend extra energy. Distract her from thinking about Simon.

Yup. She'd look into classes after Nadia was home and safe.

She'd phoned the ICU this morning. Her sister was stable and there'd been no more seizures. Kate was unchanging, according to the night shift in the NICU, though Simon's absence from the beach made that less reassuring.

She'd see Gran soon. Something about today felt positive, instead of a day spiralling down into worse and worse, and Gran was a good place to start.

'Good morning, Gran.'

Isabel placed another bowl of tiny heart-shaped

purple flowers on Gran's bedside table. This time they came with succulent leaves as well.

'Mrs Green has more violets for you.'

She glanced down at the familiar face and froze.

Her grandmother's eyes were open. Isabella shut her own eyes and held them shut for the count of three. She slowly opened them, terrified of what she'd see.

Gran's eyes were still open. They weren't vague and staring. They were lucid. And warm.

Isabella's mouth opened in wonder as two single tears slid from the corner of her grandmother's eyes.

Isabella watched, barely daring to breathe, as Gran moistened her lips and whispered hoarsely, 'Bella...'

And then she closed her eyes and drifted off. But this time there was a smile on her face.

'Gran?' Isabella called, her voice frantic. Her gaze flew to the heart rate monitor above her head and she saw the rise in the heart rate begin to settle down again from the faster rhythm to the usual seventy. She hadn't noticed it when she'd arrived.

Gran had woken up.

Spoken and been lucid.

She'd recognised Isabella.

Isabella sank into the nearest chair. She put a hand to her mouth and silent tears ran down her face.

When she lifted her head there was a nurse there. Ella—the one she saw most mornings.

'What's wrong? I saw the monitor change,'

Isabella turned damp eyes to the young woman she'd spoken to nearly every day for the last month. 'Ella… Her eyes were open. And she said my name. Then she went back to sleep.'

Isabella heard herself say the words, but even she couldn't quite believe it.

Ella nodded with delight. 'They all said I was mad when I said she was less deeply unconscious than before.' Ella reached down and quickly hugged Isabella and then stood back. 'I'm so pleased for you all, Isabella. I'll phone the doctor.'

The room quickly filled with people and Isabella found herself tucked into the corner of the room, her heart still pounding.

She needed to tell Nadia.

And her father.

But, strangely, the person she really wanted to tell was Simon.

Ella said, 'They're going to take your grandmother down to have another CAT scan. Probably other tests as well.'

Isabella understood. Ella meant she'd soon be sitting in an empty room. 'I'll leave and come back on my way to work.'

Ella nodded. 'I'll phone you if anything changes.'

'Thank you.'

Her voice cracked. Time away was probably a good idea.

She walked away, her head full of improbabilities and hope and dread all mixed up so that she could barely think. When she reached her car, she sat in it, but didn't turn on the engine. Couldn't bear to drive away.

She looked down at her phone and her fingers flew as she texted before she thought too much about it.

Gran opened her eyes, Simon. And said my name.

She sent it just like that, and a text flew back within a minute.

Where are you?

She texted back.

Sitting in my car outside the hospital. I can't seem to drive away.

His reply.

I'll be there in ten minutes.

He was there in eight. He must have run to the apartments to retrieve his vehicle. He parked three car spaces down and was out of his car and at her door faster than she would have thought possible.

He opened her door and she climbed out and into his strong, warm arms. They wrapped around her. Wrapped her with kindness, understanding, and the big-heartedness she desperately needed right at that minute.

'But what if that was her last lucid moment before she passes away?' She whispered her worst fear into his chest.

He rubbed her back. Up and down, up and down, soothing her like a child with a skinned knee.

'What if it's the beginning of her waking up properly?' he said quietly into her hair. 'I think we should go for that one. Don't you?'

The sob in Isabella's throat turned into a strangled hiccup of a laugh.

'I like your optimism,' she said. 'I desperately *need* your optimism.'

His big warm hand, still rubbing up and down her back, patted her. 'Maybe she regained consciousness because she knew you'd be here, waiting for her.'

Isabella sobbed until his shirt was wet. Big, ugly, heart-wrenching sobs of relief that she hadn't allowed herself before.

As she quieted, he pushed a big, folded square

of soft white material into her hand and she glanced at it. Her shaky laugh was a good exchange for the tears. 'I didn't think people carried handkerchiefs anymore.'

'I'm in a job where I sometimes need more than a tissue. Fragile paper just doesn't cut the mustard when your baby is sick.'

She sniffed, opened out the handkerchief, wiped her saturated eyes and cheeks, and blew her nose soundly.

He laughed. 'You can keep that.'

She offered him a wobbly grin. 'I'll wash it and give it back to you.'

He stepped away. The warmth of his hand falling away from her left a gap in her world and she missed it.

'Feel better?' he asked.

She sniffed again, but she felt as if she'd dropped a neck yoke and two full buckets off her shoulders.

'I do.'

Then she saw the way his damp shirt clung to the muscular ridges of his chest and abdomen, and suddenly she wanted nothing more than to trace the lines and hollows of his torso. She pulled her hand back as soon as it began to reach out.

'Um...you're wet. Sorry.'

'I didn't have time for a swim this morning. Must be my quota of salt water.' He was smiling, but there was heat there, too.

'Cute,' she said.

She eased away. Further. Until her back was against the closed door of the car. It felt warm from the sun, but not as warm as her belly. 'You got here quickly.'

'My friend needed me,' he said.

Friend. Cold water. That put out some of the flames.

'But I have to go back now. Are you going to be okay?' he asked.

She was used to standing on her own. But she appreciated the thought.

'Yes,' she said. 'I'll be fine. I'll go home now. I'll visit Gran again this afternoon, before I come to work.' Then another thought intruded. 'How's Kate? I was worried when you didn't come surfing.'

'The new twins are playing up. Respiratory issues. But I've pulled them into line,' he said with an easy smile.

Yet still his eyes remained serious and concerned.

About her?

'That's good. And I'm good. Now.' She met his gaze. 'Thank you, Simon. For coming when I needed you.'

His mouth opened and closed again. As if he'd thought better of what he'd been going to say. Instead, his lips formed different words. 'Have you called your father?'

No, she hadn't. She'd called *him*.

'Not yet.'

He smiled, and she suspected he liked it that she had called him first.

'I have to go. I'll see you later.' He turned towards his car, then spun back. 'Text me if you need to talk.'

CHAPTER TWENTY-SIX

SIMON LEFT ISABELLA at the hospital and his mind spun with what seemed suspiciously like delight.

She'd contacted him before her father.

To share her news and her fears. Because she'd trusted that he'd understand and be there for her.

She couldn't have known that he'd come, and he wondered what had been going on inside her head that had made her think texting him would help.

He lifted his chin as he drove back to the hospital. He had helped. Judging by her face. But when he'd first arrived—heavens, she'd looked like a fragile crystal vase about to smash into a million pieces.

He guessed she had finally broken against his chest, judging by the dampness of his skin. But the idea of Isabella—beautiful and tough and, yes, astoundingly fragile—needing him made him glad she'd called him.

In fact, the idea of Isabella seeking comfort anywhere else made his eyes narrow.

Simon wondered just how deeply he was falling for Isabella Hargraves…and if there was any hope at all that he could extricate himself before it was too late.

* * *

Simon should be in his office with his afternoon appointments, but his two-thirty had called to cancel. And instead of catching up on paperwork—which he always needed to do—he was striding through the hospital to the NICU, to be there for when Isabel started work.

He watched her push through the door, totally put-together, showing no hint of the life-altering change that had occurred for her that day. Maybe there was an extra spring in her step. Certainly there was a smile in her eyes when she saw him.

He smiled back. Must be good news with her grandmother—but he'd have to wait. She'd only just made it in time, because the shift handover was about to begin.

While he waited, he finished typing up the changes he'd made to one of the twins' treatment and checked through the notes for the rest of the tiny patients in the unit.

Fifteen minutes later the nurses had finished their walk around the patients and Isabella arrived at his side.

He was still typing on the rolling computer in front of the cot. 'Are you looking after these boys today?' he asked her.

She nodded. 'Yes.'

'Good,' he said.

They talked about the twins. Their treatment. The results of the latest blood tests. They compared thoughts on an X-ray and Simon realised he didn't even have this kind of in-depth conversation with Henry, and he was supposed to be his registrar, able to keep up.

Isabella mentioned something that might lead to a breakthrough.

He looked at her sideways. 'Good insight. I hadn't thought of that. Thank you.'

She lifted a hand, brushing it away. 'I love X-rays—they can show so much. So, you're welcome.'

He nodded, and knew he would think more on that later, but for the moment they had more important things to talk about. 'How's your grandmother?'

As he asked the question he studied her face and saw that her eyes were sparkling.

'She woke up again. She's incredibly weak, of course. But her doctor seems to think that because she recognised me and spoke again, making sense, she should just get better every day.'

'That's wonderful.' It was. Mind-blowing, really. 'Have you told Nadia?'

'Yes. I dropped into Intensive Care just before I came here. Malachi has her on some pretty strong drugs, so she's vague. But she's as thrilled as I am.'

'And your father?'

'My father told me not to expect too much.'

Simon was relieved to see she didn't look too disappointed. 'Of course he did…' Simon muttered. And then pressed his lips together. *Oops.* 'Sorry, that was judgmental.'

Isabella laughed. 'But true.'

He touched her shoulder. 'I'm very happy for you all.' *Especially you.* But he didn't say that out loud. He looked up as the phone rang and Carla called his name. 'I have to go. But I'll see you before I go home.'

He watched her beautiful mouth curve and her eyes lighten. Yes. She was glad that he'd said that. Which was good. Wasn't it…?

But Simon didn't make it back to the NICU before he went home because he spent the evening in the ICU with a young boy who'd came into Emergency with a severe asthma attack. It was touch-and-go as to whether they could save him. Simon couldn't leave the child until he was stable.

He had managed to lift his hand in a wave to Isabella when she'd entered the ICU to see Nadia. Isabella had waved back.

He finished in the ICU at ten-thirty that night, tired, rumpled, with his shirt slightly bloodstained from a tricky cannula.

On seeing the time, his first thought was Isabella, but it was too early to walk her home, and a bad time to talk to her as she prepared to end her shift and hand over. Instead, he decided to go to his own flat and shower. With luck he could walk and meet her on her way home.

Which was how he managed to find her under that first streetlight just outside the hospital, in his fresh attire and with damp skin. He'd had to rush.

Isabella met his eyes as she walked up to him. 'Fancy meeting you here.' She looked him up and down, taking in his different clothes and wet hair. 'I'm guessing you had a busy night?'

Before he could speak a huge yawn overtook him and his hand lifted to hide his cracking jaw. 'I did. But the good guys won, so that's what's important.'

She bumped his shoulder with hers. 'You're the good guy.'

Nice. He smiled at her. 'Thank you. But this good guy is exhausted.' He side-eyed her and thought, *I'm exhausted, but loving the view*. 'And starving. I didn't get dinner. Fancy sharing a late-night snack?'

'I'd like that—but how about you come to Gran's apartment? I've got some homemade pumpkin soup, half a cooked chicken and some sourdough I'm happy to share.'

'Sounds even better. What shift are you on tomorrow?' It wouldn't be fair to keep her up if she started at seven a.m.

'A two-thirty start.'

'Excellent.' And he realised as he walked along the dark street with Isabella by his side that he was very, very content.

When Simon stepped inside Catherine Hargraves' apartment his eyes skittered to the bedroom he could see through the open guest room door. The bed was made. It hadn't been before. The last time he'd seen that room Isabella had been well loved and asleep amidst tumbled sheets.

His body stirred at the memories of that night, and when he looked away he saw she'd caught the direction of his interest.

Her voice conversational, she asked, 'You regretting that?'

'Lots of emotions,' he said soberly. 'But none are regret.'

'Good.' Her gaze left his and she walked into the kitchen, as if he'd given her the right answer. 'Do you want your sourdough toasted or soft?'

CHAPTER TWENTY-SEVEN

'SOFT, PLEASE.'

Isabella turned away to hide her blushes, because she had lots of emotions about that night, too. None of them regret. And none of them soft. Mainly she felt caution, the possibility of peril, and the absolute fear of never finding another man she cared about as much as Simon.

Maybe he would change his mind.

But she was trying to keep a lid on fantasising until she heard or felt something positive back from Simon.

She understood he was wounded. Battered by the loss of his wife. And probably scared of losing another someone he might possibly build a life with. She could see why. But there had to be more.

She had her own fears. She thought about Conlon. How he'd let her down when she'd needed him most. Thought about her father and how he'd let her down so many times when she'd been desperate for a shoulder to cry on. And she thought about Simon itching to get away at breakfast the other day.

But also she remembered today. When he'd come and held her while she'd been at her most vulnerable.

Had Simon changed his mind? Let himself become more accessible to her? It did look as if he wanted her to call on him if she needed support.

Or was she dreaming the fact they were getting closer because that was what she wanted? That he might reconsider them being more than friends?

Or maybe the guy just wanted more sex since he'd broken his drought.

But she didn't think Simon was shallow, and she suspected he knew she was protecting herself from expecting more than he offered.

Which left her vulnerable again.

Maybe inviting him here tonight hadn't been her most sensible idea.

Through all these thoughts and tortured paths of indecision her hands were busy heating soup, buttering sourdough and pulling the chicken from the fridge to cut up onto a larger plate. She threw on a couple of cherry tomatoes and a handful of spinach leaves, along with a baby cucumber and sweet yellow capsicum, sliced quickly. Then she gathered a knife and fork and a bottle of mayo and put the plate down in front of him at the table.

'You start on this while the soup heats and I'll butter more toast.'

He glanced up at her. His eyes twinkled and her belly kicked.

'So...you're one of those women who can make something out of nothing in less than two minutes?'

Stick to this conversation.

'I've had years of grabbing quick snacks. And I don't like commercial fast food, so I always have the makings.'

Simon opened his eyes wide. 'You don't like fast food? Wash your mouth out.' He reached for the plate and the cutlery.

He laughed and ate, and by the time she brought out the toast and soup he was scraping the plate.

'Hungry, much?'

'I have been wasting away,' he acknowledged, as she put a blue mug filled with steaming soup beside him, along with a plate holding two big slices of sourdough and real butter.

She considered his wide shoulders, gloriously broad chest—and those arms! *Oh, my.* This man was *not* wasting away.

Luckily, Simon missed her long, hungry examination as he looked at the soup with eager anticipation. 'Now I might live.'

Smiling, damping down the fire that had burst into flame in her belly, she went back into the kitchen and returned with her own soup and bread. She sat down opposite him. 'So? What happened in ICU?'

He was the one who was strung up this time. She, for a change, was feeling calm—or as calm as she could be with Simon across the table from her late at night, looking scrumptious. It was a nice change from her meltdown against that particular awesome chest earlier today.

But she had a feeling he'd had some trauma that still bothered him. Horrors lingering after the close call she'd heard about tonight, when one of the ICU nurses had spoken to her during her break with Nadia.

'Was it the young boy? Arlo? Asthma?'

Simon shook his head. 'Horrid disease. I hate it. Sometimes they get so shut down you just can't break through to their lungs.' He blew out a big sigh. 'We were lucky. We managed in the end.'

'Good job.'

He shook his head. 'I still can't believe the kid didn't even have an asthma plan for his mum to work through if he started to get sick. I'll have to contact his GP. Have a word with the practice about patient safety with asthmatics.'

She listened as he ranted a little. And then talked about the scariest bits. The fact that the boy's eyes had watched him, terrified, as he'd struggled for breath, and how Simon had thought he'd been going to lose him. And that wasn't even mentioning the distraught parents.

'But we won,' he finished, as if it had been a huge battle.

She could see that it had been. 'They were lucky to have you,' she said.

'It took a team,' he said. And looked away.

He seemed uncomfortable with the praise, and she wondered about his childhood. About his inability to take a compliment graciously. Not losing a patient seemed vitally, intrinsically imperative to him. It was the end goal for all health professionals, but to Simon it seemed more. As if his own life and death was in the balance.

'I'm lucky to have you to listen to me. And feed me. That was delicious.'

They'd both finished, and the empty plates had been pushed to the middle of the table.

Suddenly it felt as if the air had been sucked from the room. Which was crazy, because she had the door to the balcony open and the curtains were floating in a soft sea breeze.

She licked her suddenly dry lips. 'You should go to bed, Simon.' She stood up. 'You need to sleep.'

He rose, and Isabella walked towards the door. He followed her closely—which was good, wasn't it? But so was the fact that before she could undo the lock he had rested his hand on her shoulder and turned her to face him.

Yes. She wanted this.

Stepping close, he put both hands above her head against the door. Caging her loosely. But not holding her.

As he gazed down into her face she knew she should slip under his arm and away, but there was a lot of heat coming from his body that was now so close to hers. And she liked that heat. All she had to do was say the word, though, and she knew he would let her go.

But that was hard to do when she didn't want to.

'Is this a friends-with-benefits moment?'

He winced. He lowered his face, resting his forehead against hers. 'I don't know what this is.' Then he straightened, kissed her very gently on the lips before he pulled back. 'But right now I think I want to find out.'

His lips had been warm…seeking and offering. But his words stopped her.

They made Isabella lift her chin higher and move her head towards the door a little, increasing the gap between them.

She caught and held his gaze, her eyes narrowing. 'Are you sure about that Simon?'

There was challenge in her words…regret in her stomach. Because she knew how this would end. 'Because "I think I want to find out" isn't good enough.'

She scooted under his arm and put some distance between them before she did something that she, and apparently he, would regret.

'Nowhere near good enough. You should get some sleep. Goodnight.'

CHAPTER TWENTY-EIGHT

SIMON FELT THE absence of Isabella as she moved out of his reach like a gap in the universe. How had it come to this so quickly? So quickly that his head spun?

While his sense of loss urged him to answer her question the way she wanted, he knew that wouldn't be fair. Because it was true. He was still thinking about this. And he was a fool for pushing it.

'Thank you for being the sensible one,' he said.

He moved his hands from the door where she'd been. Returned them to his sides.

'Good call, Isabella. I need to sleep.'

He reached forward, opened the door, and let himself out before he could promise something he still wasn't convinced was true.

All the way back to his apartment he remembered her face, and the narrowing of her beautiful eyes as she demanded an honest answer.

She was amazing. Incredible. A way more put-together person than he was. Hell, he probably didn't deserve her anyway.

His father had said he wouldn't amount to much. And that parting sneer had driven Simon out of the only home he'd known to push himself at his studies until he could prove the man wrong.

The old martinet had died before Simon had been admitted to med school, which had left Simon a little skewed about his self-worth. But he'd hung out with the other misfit in college—Malachi Madden—and together they'd been a force to be reckoned with. The bond that had grown between them had turned out to be rock-solid, and Malachi—the brother he'd never had—always had his back.

Was his lack of self-worth stopping him? Was that why he was holding back from Isabella? He didn't know. Maybe he'd ask his pseudo-brother tomorrow. Because Malachi had been worse at relationships than he was—until Lisandra had taken control.

Simon woke at dawn. For once, his phone hadn't gone off overnight. He jerked on his board shorts and grabbed his board. If he hadn't had two metres of fibreglass under his arm he would have jogged down the fire escape, to get a bit more exercise. But surfboards and narrow stairwells didn't go well together.

As he stepped out into the dim, cool morning, he breathed in the fresh salt air and decided to stop beating himself up about his vacillations over Isabella.

It would take as long as it took for him to get over his bereavement…be normal again.

In fact, he had come a long way towards 'normal' since Isabella Hargraves had first smashed through his barriers nearly five weeks ago.

Had it even been five weeks?

She'd been like a steamroller through the barriers that he'd thought impervious. She'd pushed through his defences as if they were putty.

And that had been just her looks.

Her brilliant brain blew him away, too.

He thought about the way they were so synchronised in their thought processes when discussing sick babies and possible prognoses. That was hot too.

Then he'd seen the big family-centred heart of her and he'd been a goner.

A goner? *Was* he a goner?

He thought about the way she caught his eye every time she moved. He thought about the softness of her skin against his. Glorious. And she knew karate. His mouth kinked up. He wanted to explore that!

But questions and commitments and answers were all in play, and he couldn't go through another heartbreak. His father was right. He couldn't even keep the people he cared about safe. And Isabella didn't deserve the kind of person he was.

Simon walked into Malachi's office at eight-thirty, with his hair still wet from his post-surf shower.

There'd used to be days when Malachi was there at seven a.m., but family life had trained him out of that. Now the man even left before five in the evening some nights. Simon wasn't quite sure how Lisandra had achieved that, but there was no doubt that Dr Madden had more balance in his life now than Simon had.

Malachi looked up to see him at the door and raised his brows. 'What are you doing here?'

'Lovely greeting for your best friend.'

'*Only* friend apart from my darling wife.'

That was probably true. 'I've come for advice.'

The twinkle that materialised more and more often in his friend's eyes made Simon feel as if his ears were burning.

'You've fallen for Isabella!' Malachi appeared disgustingly delighted.

It wasn't a question. He hadn't even had to explain. Which was a relief of sorts.

'Not like you to be so observant, Malachi.

He shrugged. 'Lisandra told me.' It was a statement of fact.

Simon sighed. Of course she had.

'Thing is, I don't know if I want to do that whole *I would lose my world if anything happened to her* scenario.'

'You're scared.'

Malachi was known for his straight shooting. And for his ability to miss the concept of tactful advice. That was why he'd come here, wasn't it? Maybe…

Malachi sat down at his desk and leaned back in his chair. 'How long have you known her?'

'Less than five weeks.'

'Plenty,' said his now superior friend. 'Even I, stunted relationship guru that I was, only took a week to realise that Lisandra was the one I didn't want to get away.'

'You're saying take the risk? Put myself out on a limb?'

Malachi arched a brow. 'You won't be out on the limb by yourself. Isabella will be there. But you're the only one who knows whether you're ready, Simon. Lisandra says you've taken too long as it is.'

His friend tilted his head at him and shooed him out of his office.

'Get a move on.'

CHAPTER TWENTY-NINE

AFTER ANOTHER BUSY SHIFT, with two new prem babies admitted to the NICU and Kate improving, Isabella finished work and stepped out into the night with a smile. She wasn't surprised to see Simon under the streetlight outside.

'We really have to stop meeting like this,' she quipped.

It was funny, considering they'd spent about four hours together on and off throughout her shift.

'Was there something you couldn't tell me in the middle of the NICU?'

He didn't answer her facetious question. Instead, he said, 'I've started to really like this time of night.'

'Really? Angling for another invite? Well, I'm on the morning shift tomorrow. No midnight snacks for you.'

He smiled easily. Which meant he hadn't been expecting that scenario but had decided to come and meet her anyway. Curiouser and curiouser…

He glanced up at the moon overhead. 'That's okay. I just thought I'd walk you home.'

'Thank you. I may be your *friend…*' she emphasised the word '…but I don't need protecting. You know that, right?'

He looked struck for a moment, and she wasn't sure why. But then he went off on another tangent. 'I see Malachi is transferring Nadia back to the ward again tomorrow.'

She thought about her sister's excellent progress and it sat well. Such relief.

'Yes. He's pretty sure she'll be fine this time. She's still on heavy-duty antihypertensives, but at least the blood pressure is staying down now.'

'And I assume you'll be happy that Kate's back on oral feeds tomorrow?'

'I am.'

She wasn't making it easy for him, which wasn't like her, but Isabella was still a wee bit irritated about last night. Her mind had circled around Simon's intentions. What were they if he didn't feel that there was a relationship in the future for them? Just sex?

Today, when they worked together, they'd both remained very professional. Even Carla hadn't made any cheeky comments. So why was he here? Apart from his notion that near-midnight rambling was a pleasant idea.

'I didn't get a chance to ask—how's Catherine? Has there been more progress??'

Her crossness evaporated. She loved the way he called her grandmother by her name. Highlighting that he saw her as a person, not just as a patient recovering from a head injury or, as in her father's case, a hopeless invalid. She appreciated that subtext of support more than he probably knew.

Relief and pleasure rolled over her as she thought about Gran. 'She was sitting up today. In the chair. Not for long, but they've stopped the parenteral nutrition and she's drinking and eating soft foods.'

'That's amazing.' His delight seemed genuine, and she hugged that to herself.

'That's what the doctors are saying. They can't believe how fast she's recovering. Even Dad's gobsmacked. He's flying up at the weekend to see her.'

'I really am thrilled.'

And his smile, which was pleased for her as well as Gran, warmed her more.

'Nadia might even be discharged by then,' he added.

'I know. My world is changing. Things are finally going right.'

She should not have said that.

They were almost at the apartments, and up ahead she could see a man sitting on the low wall at the front of the block. She was glad that Simon was beside her.

Simon saw the figure as well, and stiffened. He stepped closer, until his shoulder touched hers.

As they neared, the man stood up. She recognised him. Though he seemed smaller. Slighter. Compared to Simon. Her light-heartedness disappeared. So much for everything going right for a change.

'Conlon. Hello. What are you doing here?'

She felt Simon's stillness. Did he remember her mentioning him?

Her ex glanced at Simon, and then back at her. His brow furrowed. 'I flew into Brisbane. You didn't answer my texts.' It sounded like a complaint not a statement.

She felt Simon relax slightly beside her.

Conlon was whining on. 'Your father said you were finishing at eleven and gave me your address.'

Still whining. Had he always whined?

Isabella closed her eyes for a moment. *Thanks, Dad.* She could feel Simon looming beside her, radiating distrust and other emotions. She wondered what he saw when he looked at Conlon. Judging by the expression on his face, not something he liked.

'Simon, this is Dr Conlon Brazier. We were working on a scientific paper together in Hanoi. Conlon, this is Dr Simon Purdy. Simon is walking me home in the dark.'

Conlon put his hand out. 'Great idea. Thanks for that.'

Simon jammed his hands in his pockets. The action quite forcible, as if had he not performed it, he might do something he regretted. 'Didn't do it for you, mate.'

Isabella suppressed a smile. 'No, you did it for me.' She looked up at him and smiled. 'Thank you, Simon. But I'll be fine now.'

She thought for a moment that Simon wasn't going to leave, but he nodded, stalked into the porch to unlock the door, and disappeared. The door didn't click shut behind him, staying open a crack. She suspected Simon was making sure Conlon wasn't going to annoy her.

She hid her smile. Her over-protective friend. That said more about Simon than he probably realised.

Had Simon been jealous? She'd think about that later.

First, she had to shake off her ex. Permanently.

'I'm on a morning shift tomorrow, Conlon. There's no need for us to talk. Anything between us is well and truly over.'

Conlon came closer. Into her space. *Idiot.*

'We had something, Isabella. We were good together in Vietnam.'

She stared into his arrogant, handsome face with a coolness she wouldn't have believed possible a month ago.

'Maybe. Briefly. But…' She shook her head as if msystified. 'It's gone now.'

She shrugged and saw him flinch. She wanted no misunderstandings. No comebacks. She doubted it had ever been more than superficial, now that she knew what real, world-shaking attraction, lust and magnetic draw was. Like she had for Simon.

She resisted a glance towards the door he'd disappeared through.

Conlon eased closer. 'I should have been more supportive. I'll try to do better. I flew all this way to see you.'

Yep. Whining.

'Conlon. Not happening. You let me down when I needed you. There's no going back.'

Isabella stepped past him—though really she wanted to push him onto his backside. Instead, she huffed out a small puff of amusement. He'd just think she accidentally shoved him. The guy was oblivious.

She said, with finality, 'It's been a big week for me, and I desperately need sleep. You can go now.'

His horrified eyes widened. 'You're just going to leave me out in the cold?'

She almost laughed. Except none of this was funny. 'It's the Gold Coast, Conlon. Twenty degrees Celsius.'

He huffed in disgust. 'I hoped you'd at least put me up.'

She teetered for a moment. Maybe she should take him in? They had been more than friends. But then common sense flooded back, and a wave of tiredness over the top of the shock of seeing him. Unannounced. Unwanted. Unsupportive Conlon.

No.

'You're a big boy. The airport hotel has twenty-four-hour check-in. That's where Dad stays when he's up here. I'm surprised he didn't tell you that.'

Conlon had the grace to look slightly embarrassed. 'He did.'

'I *would* drive you, but I'm done. Call a taxi—they respond fast here. Do you want me to wait here with you?'

'Not if you're too tired to talk to me.'

Sarcastic and definitely with the assumption that she would stay, and he'd keep trying, Isabella decided.

He'd be fine. 'Excellent. Goodnight.'

How had she ever thought she had a future with this petulant man?

She turned and left him, relief expanding inside her as she walked away. Simon wasn't behind the door inside, but the lift was still going up. He had just been there. She smiled.

Riding up in the elevator herself, Isabella felt briefly tempted to keep going all the way to the top and tell Simon that she and Conlon had no future. Ever. But Simon… Well, Simon was still *thinking* he wanted to find out what could grow between them.

Let him think about Conlon. She really was tired.

At last Isabella allowed herself to acknowledge the strain of the last weeks.

Tonight, seeing Conlon, she'd remembered the first moment her father had called her in Hanoi to tell her of Gran's accident.

She hadn't had any support as she'd rushed to Gran's side. And she'd had to be the strong one and drag Nadia to the emergency department when she'd suspected pre-eclampsia.

It was her belligerence that had requested Simon's consultancy when Kate was born.

She'd even refused to believe her father's dire prognosis, and stayed with the faith Gran would wake.

Now that Gran was improving, Isabella wanted to stand down. Stop being the rock, always on her own against the odds.

But maybe she wasn't truly on her own anymore.

Simon had stepped up.

He'd taken over with Kate, ensuring her excellent care.

He'd been her sounding board when her father had let her down, as usual.

He'd been there when Nadia had been readmitted to the ICU and Isabella had been so scared.

Most of all she remembered him driving fast to the hospital, when Gran had opened her eyes and Isabella had melted down against his shirt.

The elevator doors opened.

There, beside her front door, stood Simon.

Despite the fact that she'd just decided he could stew in his own juices, it was good to see him. Wonderful.

She couldn't help the crooked smile she gave him. 'Fancy meeting you here,' she said, echoing the earlier greeting. She crossed the hallway to him.

'I'm sorry,' he said. 'I was a jealous idiot downstairs and I behaved badly. And I eavesdropped.'

She looked at him. Blond. Strong and beautiful. Hopefully hers.

She touched his cheek. 'Don't bother worrying. He won't be coming back.'

'Why is that?' Simon asked, but she saw that he knew.

'You were listening?'

'In case you needed me.'

'I didn't.'

'I heard that.'

The relief in his eyes shone plainly. Along with a furnace of heat.

'Because he let me down.' This was important. It had to be said. 'That's the one thing I won't have from the man in my life. Never again.'

Simon stepped closer. 'And if I promise not to let you down?'

'There's no "if", Simon. *Do* you promise that?'

His chin went high. He lifted his hand to his heart to rest on his chest. 'Yes.'

His voice was firm. His eyes held hers. There was no doubting the sincerity. The inherent promise.

'If you'll let me into your life?'

'I know—I don't *think*,' she said, using words ironically, because he'd used them last night, 'that you're already in my life, Simon. You're the one who needs to remember that I'm in yours.'

She passed him and put her key in the lock and slipped away.

The door closed behind her.

CHAPTER THIRTY

SIMON STOOD OUTSIDE Isabella's door and thought about knocking. Asking her what she meant.

He imagined kissing her.

Then he thought about the tiredness in her eyes and in the droop of her shoulders.

Shook his head. No. Not tonight.

He played back what she'd said about Conlon—that he would never come back after today. He'd heard that dismissal. *Ouch.* Okay, then. He acknowledged the fact that she was willing to trust that he would never let her down if she let him in. That she'd said he was a part of her life.

She'd also said he needed to realise she was a part of his.

Suddenly it wasn't hard to be certain that he wanted Isabella Hargraves in his life—for now and for always.

The other thing he'd come to realise—painful, but true, and just a bit enlightening—was that Isabella didn't need his protection. She would protect herself. In fact, he thought with a smile, she could probably protect *him*.

She didn't want protection. She wanted a partnership. With him. She wanted support as an individual. But with him.

His darling Louise had always been soft. Gentle. In need of protection. Thus, when she'd died, his soul had whispered that he was the one at fault for not protecting her.

That whisper had coiled around him, merged with the guilt his father had left him with, and stolen his smile. His faith in himself. He'd built up his walls so that he could never fail to protect anyone ever again. Those conjoined whispers had kept him from trusting his heart to find someone he wouldn't let down.

Isabella had restored his faith. Isabella didn't want protection. She wanted a man at her back as well as by her side. Through thick and thin. She wanted him, and he had no idea how he could have been so lucky.

He could do what she needed. Because it was what he needed too. He wanted to be there always for the woman he loved.

He loved her. She'd been a wrecking ball he hadn't expected—stealing his breath and his heart.

He'd been finding his self-esteem in protecting his patients. Being there for them twenty-four-seven at work had given his life meaning. What Isabella offered was so much more than that…so much more sustainable.

Maybe now he could understand his friend's soul-deep happiness. And his advice to get a move on.

It was time to start wooing his love. Building

trust. To ensure that his Isabella knew he would always be there for her. Proud to be by her side.

The next afternoon, late in the day, as he walked back into the unit, Simon acknowledged that it had been a good day. He and Isabella had a professional working relationship that ran smoothly, and he was planning to court her with his charms when work was behind them. He even had a plan.

Nadia had moved back to the ward and was looking well. Simon felt pleased for her, and Kate, but also for Isabella, who had been so worried about her sister.

Malachi had assured him that Nadia would continue to improve now, as all her blood results had settled down—Simon had checked with him so he could reassure Isabella if she needed more.

Kate was back on tube feeds, and had had her first skin-to-skin kangaroo care with her mother, tucked under her mum's shirt against her bare skin.

He'd gone down to the unit for the event, and had smiled with everyone else when Kate was settled, with her head poking out of her mother's shirt. He'd been watching Isabella the most, and the joy he'd seen on her face had warmed his heart and filled him somewhere he hadn't realised he'd been empty.

There'd been three babies discharged from the unit as well, going home happy and healthy.

With those babies gone suddenly there was time to breathe—until the next rush of patients arrived. These moments gave the dedicated staff time to be satisfied with the job they were doing, caring for their tiny charges.

He'd timed his return to the unit now for just before Isabella walked out through the door. He caught her as she was saying goodbye to her niece and she didn't see him coming.

He touched her shoulder. 'I know you don't have to see Big Boy Conlon when you finish here…'

She flashed a grin at him, remembering that she'd told Conlon he was a big boy and could find himself somewhere else to sleep. 'Funny man…'

He smiled. 'Well, I used to be a funny man. And I'm finding humour again. Because there's this woman I fancy so much that I'm willing to change. And Carla tells me the sadness I've been wallowing in has grown really old.'

She smiled at that too. Watching his face with that careful attention she gave to anyone she spoke to.

'But that's not why I'm here,' he said.

'Goodness,' she said—a little facetiously, he thought. 'Why *are* you here?'

'Anyway,' he continued quietly, 'when you leave here, are you going to visit Catherine?'

'Yes.' Those lovely brows arched. 'Why?'

'Would you mind if I came? You could text me and I could meet you there.'

He wasn't sure what he would do if she said no.

She tilted her head at him. 'Sure. I can leave at five.'

'Great. I'll be on time.'

She looked startled and pleased. Good. He'd ticked one box on his mental list.

'And afterwards…' He tried a winning smile and her lips twitched. 'I'd like to take you on a dinner date.'

'A date?' she said. 'Haven't we moved past that?'

'Not officially.'

She cocked her head. 'We've had breakfast together… I've met your friends…we've had dinner…' She waggled her brows. 'And more!'

'Yes, but this is me asking you to dress up and come out to a flash meal with me for the purpose of getting to know each other better. With nobody else present.'

'Simon Purdy—' she started, but Carla had crossed the room to them with a small piece of paper for Simon and she stopped.

'Yes, I know,' he said. 'We'll talk about it tonight.'

He saluted her and turned to Carla.

And that was how he ended up at the hospital just after five.

Now that he really observed Catherine Hargraves, he decided she looked like he imagined Isabella would look in fifty years. Snow-white hair had been brushed back off her face in soft waves. She had a long neck, like her granddaughter, and the same angled cheekbones and the same large green eyes, though faded.

But mostly it was the bright mind lurking at the back of those eyes that made him think of Isabella.

He picked up the wrinkled hand, stroked his thumb over the soft skin and bowed over it.

'Mrs Hargraves… You're obviously made of stern stuff,' he said. 'It's wonderful to see you looking so alert.'

'As opposed to comatose?' she said, a quirk of amusement tilting her mouth.

'Isabella never gave up on you,' he said.

'No. She didn't.'

He watched Catherine Hargraves glance at her granddaughter.

'She's a strong woman. She's had to be.'

There it was. That mutual appreciation between Isabella and her grandmother. A precious thing that he envied.

'I know,' he said softly.

He squeezed her hand gently, rested it back on the covers and stepped back.

Isabella had been talking to the doctor at the door, discussing discharge dates and reminding the doctor that she lived with her grandmother and would be able to help with the heavier tasks that might be difficult for her at the moment.

When she returned to the bedside her smile was reflected in her eyes. 'Possibly Monday. How do you feel about that, Gran?'

'Sounds fine.'

'Great! I'm off Tuesday and Wednesday. I could pick you up after work Monday afternoon. Then we'd have two full days together.'

Her grandmother pretended to slump in exhaustion against the pillows. Or most of it was pretend. 'Not full days, child. Your energy would drive me batty.'

'I'll take her off your hands when she's too much, Catherine. Just let me know.'

Simon watched Isabella's face as he said it, and saw how she tucked in her chin and looked at him from under her brows.

'Will you, now?' she asked.

'Surf, sand and avocado on rye as necessary,' he agreed. 'But now I think I've stayed long enough. I'll wait for you at your car. No hurry.'

He watched Isabella shoot a quick glance at her grandmother. 'No. I'll come too. We've both stayed long enough.'

Which was what he'd hoped she'd say. Because he knew that even in Isabella's excitement she would not have missed the droop of exhaustion in the older woman's shoulders. But he didn't think she'd mind him creating the opportunity to leave.

As they walked out onto the street, he said, 'So…? Dinner? Do you like Greek?'

'I love Greek food.'

'Is seven p.m. enough time for you?'

He couldn't wait.

'Sure.'

'I'll pick you up at six forty-five. We'll take my car.'

She laughed, and her face filled his vision. She leaned in and kissed him. She tasted of sunshine and mint. 'You haven't got over that yet. Have you?'

Her mouth against his made him melt. But this wasn't the place. Or the time.

Instead he said, 'Smart Alec.' She filled him with joy.

'I'm willing to be persuaded to take your vehicle occasionally, but you'll need a good argument,' she told him.

He wondered if even Hanoi traffic had fazed Isabella.

She patted his arm. 'You can be the driver tonight.'

CHAPTER THIRTY-ONE

SIMON BROUGHT FLOWERS. Wildflowers. Her favourite kind. A huge bunch of beautiful proteas, flannel flowers, waratahs and everlasting daisies.

The armful lay against his white shirt like a frame for his smile until he handed it over. The bouquet almost sang with exuberance—glorious and perfectly set off by native leaves and grasses.

'So beautiful… And they will still look gorgeous when Gran comes home.'

'I thought about that,' he said, smiling around his pleasure at her obvious approval.

'That's thoughtful.' He *was* thoughtful.

'Thank you.'

He had no idea how much she appreciated his kindness.

'I love them.'

And she knew, now that she'd allowed her dreams to surface, how much she loved *him*.

His expression—the tilt of his stubborn chin and the beautiful smile on his face—said how pleased he felt as he watched her reaction.

He slid a small blue paper packet out of his pocket. 'I also brought chocolates.'

This was a real date, then. The whole hog.

She widened her eyes at him. 'Thank you. I

love chocolates. As long as you help me eat them later.'

His eyes said he could do more than that.

Oh, my.

His lips formed the words. 'I can do that.'

She nodded for him to put them on the table while she took the flowers into the kitchen and hugged them to herself. She breathed them in to steady the excitement that had ramped up since he arrived. Her date really was pulling out all the stops. She wondered if she should thank Conlon for Simon's over-eagerness to pursue her and suppressed a grin.

She pulled the largest vase from under the sink and filled it with water. 'I'll pop the whole lot in here until later, and sort them out when we come home.'

She heard the echo of those words…*when we come home*. Presumptuous—maybe ambitious—but her belly kicked in anticipation.

Simon must have caught on to the concept, too, because his eyes darkened. 'We should go now…'

His voice had dropped to that deeper, hungry, gravelly tone she was coming to recognise.

'Or we'll be late.'

She glanced up at him. Saw the craving, heard the unspoken *really late*, and smiled as she grabbed her small clutch with her keys inside.

She said a little breathlessly, 'Coming.'

They didn't speak on the way to the restaurant, but the car simmered like a pot on the stove with the unspoken heat between them. His shoulder and hers were close, and buzzing even without touching.

The restaurant had dressed itself in blue and white, which was funny because Simon was wearing a white shirt and she was wearing an Aegean-blue trouser suit in silk.

'You look beautiful,' he murmured. 'Did you get that in Vietnam?'

'Thank you. And, yes, I did. My friend is a tailor there, and she kept pushing them on me after I nursed her son. We're very colour co-ordinated in here.'

He lifted his glass to her.

They'd ordered two flutes of sparkling Greek rosé and they clinked crystal in a toast.

'To the future,' he said.

'The future…' she murmured.

That was…unexpected. And bold. She met his eyes and sipped. She tasted the explosion of fruit in the underlying rose petals and set the glass down.

'Lovely wine.'

'Malachi tells me it's Lisandra's favourite. I thought you might like it.'

'I do.'

So he'd discussed this dinner with his friend. Interesting… Very interesting.

'What else did you discuss with Malachi Madden?'

'Apparently, Lisandra told him I was taking too long to make a move on you.'

Isabella spluttered, glad her wine was on the table. 'Did she, now? I'll tease her about that when I see her next.'

His hand reached across the table and captured her fingers in his. 'I was a fool the other night. I don't want to be a fool again. I'm moving now. Forward, I hope. Not letting go.'

The dinner passed in a blur of heated glances, brushing fingers and hot knees touching beneath the table.

Isabella didn't remember much about the food. She remembered the wine, because the cool touch of the glass against her lips put out some of the heat from Simon's gaze. His hot, hungry gaze that rested so often on her mouth…

When she opened the door to her grandmother's apartment, he backed her into the room and pulled the door handle from her fingers gently. He didn't turn on the light, letting the glow from the moon be the only illumination in the room.

She'd left the curtains open and moonglow spilled across his face. It turned him into a silver god, and her into a woman so very willing to surrender.

His hand captured the back of her neck, warm and possessive. The other cupped her cheek as he leaned her against the wall.

'Do you have any idea how much I want you?'

His words caressed her skin, murmured against her throat, heating her nerves from throat to toes. His dark, dark eyes drilled into hers with such awe and possessive need. She hadn't dreamt that so much wanton, fiery desire would ever be directed at her.

She waved her hand in front of her face. 'There's a lot of heat coming from you,' she whispered. 'Perhaps we'll both burst into flames.'

The idea had merit.

Simon growled, 'I'd like to find out. You know I'll want you for ever? You up for that?'

'I was hoping…'

And that was the last almost full sentence she managed to utter for a very long time.

CHAPTER THIRTY-TWO

Three months later

ON THE MORNING of Simon and Isabella's wedding, Isabella watched the last of the wedding preparations from her bedroom in Gran's apartment. The temporary lights set up on the beach allowed the wedding planners to scoot around and set up before sunrise.

The path to the beach held an avenue of tall white wedding flags with silver hearts dangling from their ends. Isabella would walk through them and the newlyweds would return that way.

The sand hadn't found its sunlit gold yet, and the still, indigo ocean lay flat, a lazy mini swell all that hinted at the possibilities Lady Ocean could offer. Later she would glitter and spin with the sunlight under the gentle breeze.

Down at the water's edge and to one side, a huge white circular umbrella gently flapped, tipped with the same silver hearts dangling from each flag. The umbrella was planted above a white table covered in the same material, flanked by potted palm trees. Two pristine deckchairs waited for after the ceremony, when Simon and Isabella would sit and sign the marriage certificate.

Five rows of white chairs, four each side of the aisle, waited for the guests. More palm trees in pots graced each row on the outside edge.

The whole thing was likc a tiny chapel at the edge of the sea.

Isabella blinked back unexpected prickles in her eyes. *Stop it. No time to redo mascara.* But the setting below had sprung up even more beautifully than she'd imagined, and would look wonderful when the sun rose.

'Isabella? Darling, nearly time to go.'

Her grandmother stood at the door in a pale turquoise sheath. Her eyes were clear and bright. She had recovered most of her vigour and all of her sharp wit.

'You look beautiful, Gran,' Isabella said as her grandmother came into the room.

Gran's make-up lay perfectly, and her white hair, professionally styled, was soft about her face.

Isabella knew that Lisandra had been the instigator of quite an organisational campaign in the early hours, from five a.m., when a team of stylists and make-up artists had arrived to prepare the wedding party.

Catherine murmured, 'You look beautiful in white, darling. You should wear it more often.'

Isabella glanced down at the floor-length sheath, studded at neck and hemline with the luminous pearls that her seamstress friend from Hanoi had wanted to sew on as a gift.

'Thank you.'

The long slit that ran to Isabella's tanned thigh would make her walk up the sandy aisle easy. Her feet were encased in tiny silver slip-ons which she would leave at the edge of the sand and go barefoot—she and Simon wanted to be the only ones who would go unshod.

'I never imagined myself in a white wedding dress, Gran…'

'And why not? Today is the start of your beautiful life with Simon. Mutual love such as yours should be celebrated with distinction.'

Distinction? Yes. Her gorgeous, generous Simon deserved distinction. Their joy in each other had grown and spread like foam on the ocean, diffusing through their world and reaching out to bubble into everything. And everyone. Even her father looked happier sometimes.

She loved Simon so much…admired him, delighted in his brilliant brain, and in his quirky sense of humour that still caught her at unexpected intervals and seemed to grow each day. She loved him so much she couldn't imagine not having him by her side. At her back. In her bed. For ever.

Two more figures crowded at the door. Nadia in cornflower-blue and Lisandra in lapis lazuli.

Her three matrons of honour matched the shifting blues of the ocean. Each carried a small spray of multi-shaded blue flowers, with baby's breath backed by blue-green gum leaves, and wore silver slip-on sandals like Isabella's.

She'd wanted to be there before dawn, when the beach colours were the most ethereal, but they'd compromised for the non-morning people and had gone for sunrise instead.

It had taken three months for Catherine Hargraves to re-establish her strength well enough to be able to enjoy a wedding as a principal player, and Isabella and Simon had waited patiently for her grandmother to be one of the bridal party.

Now it was time.

Professor Piers Hargraves appeared at the door, with a serious face that said he couldn't see any good coming out of this match. The women in the room glanced at each other and pressed their painted lips together.

'For goodness' sake, Piers! It's a wedding, not a funeral. Smile!' his mother ordered.

Isabella had to stifle a laugh. The more time she spent with Simon, the less her father's dourness affected her. Simon had helped her realise that her dad's emotional distance was his default. And not her fault. It didn't matter. She still loved him, despite all his doom and gloom. But that didn't stop her winking at her grandmother.

* * *

Simon stood barefoot at the edge of the water, watching the path through the flags for the woman he loved.

'She'd better hurry or we're here early for nothing and we'll miss the sunrise,' Malachi murmured sagely. He had shoes on.

Simon shook his head. 'She won't be late.'

Just then the music began—gentle flutes playing the 'Bridal March' in the morning air, the notes soaring and sweeping like the gulls above.

The first of the bride's attendants swayed into view and he heard Malachi suck in a breath. When he glanced at his best man, he saw Malachi's attention was focussed fully on his wife. Lisandra swayed onwards, in a dress coloured with the shifting, vibrant blue of a lapis stone.

'So beautiful…' his friend sighed.

There was an amused huff from Simon. 'You're supposed to be supporting me.'

Malachi flicked him a glance, and then his gaze ricocheted unerringly back to his wife. 'Don't need to. I'm surplus. You've got this.'

Nadia sashayed into view. Isabella's sister looked so good in a dress the paler blue of a cloudless afternoon sky.

Then came Catherine, slow and gracious, in her dress which was the turquoise of ocean shallows in the sunshine.

Isabella had told him she'd chosen the colours because those were what she saw when they were out on their boards. So fitting. So beautiful. So deep and thoughtful, his Isabella…

Catherine looked well, and the rosy bloom of her now healthy skin colour made him think briefly of the unexpected delight of his being treated by her like a favourite grandchild.

But the sky was getting lighter.

Sunrise was approaching.

And finally he saw a figure in white. His Isabella. His future. The woman who held his heart in her sure hands and promised him a partnership he'd never even dreamed was possible.

His chest tightened as his vibrant, joyful bride—so vital, like the first day he saw her, his Isabella—came closer. She slipped off her sandals and stepped on to the sand.

She'd said having bare feet together meant the beginning of a promise…casting off the world to come together bare of protection, open to the sand below their feet. Connected to each other and only each other, with their bare feet joined in the golden grains that had been there for millennia.

He loved her so much.

Emotion swelled. His eyes prickled and he blinked away the sting of tears at the memory of her serious, heartfelt explanation.

Their gazes met and she smiled just for him,

her face lighting with love and excitement and the *joie de vivre* that was so much a part of the woman he'd fallen in love with that first day.

He reached out his hand and finally her precious fingers slid into his palm as they entwined their fingers and their lives for ever.

* * * * *

If you enjoyed this story, check out these other great reads from Fiona McArthur

Father for the Midwife's Twins
Taking a Chance on the Best Man
Second Chance in Barcelona
The Midwife's Secret Child

All available now!